Samuel French Acting Edition

Centennial Casting

by Gino DiIorio
& Nancy Bleemer

I0591865

‖ SAMUEL FRENCH ‖
SAMUELFRENCH.COM **SAMUELFRENCH.CO.UK**

FOR PRODUCTION ENQUIRIES

UNITED STATES AND CANADA
Info@SamuelFrench.com
1-866-598-8449

UNITED KINGDOM AND EUROPE
Plays@SamuelFrench.co.uk
020-7255-4302

Each title is subject to availability from Samuel French, depending upon country of performance. Please be aware that *CENTENNIAL CASTING* may not be licensed by Samuel French in your territory. Professional and amateur producers should contact the nearest Samuel French office or licensing partner to verify availability.

MUSIC USE NOTE

Licensees are solely responsible for obtaining formal written permission from copyright owners to use copyrighted music in the performance of this play and are strongly cautioned to do so. If no such permission is obtained by the licensee, then the licensee must use only original music that the licensee owns and controls. Licensees are solely responsible and liable for all music clearances and shall indemnify the copyright owners of the play(s) and their licensing agent, Samuel French, against any costs, expenses, losses and liabilities arising from the use of music by licensees. Please contact the appropriate music licensing authority in your territory for the rights to any incidental music.

IMPORTANT BILLING AND CREDIT REQUIREMENTS

If you have obtained performance rights to this title, please refer to your licensing agreement for important billing and credit requirements.

CENTENNIAL CASTING was first produced by Penguin Rep Theatre, Stony Point, New York on June 30, 2006. The performance was directed by Joe Brancato, with sets by James Dardenne, costumes by Cheryl McCarron, sound design by Mark Goodloe, and lighting design by Peter F. Petrino. The production stage manager was Jack D. McDowell. The cast was as follows:

VINCENT DIDONATO .... Lou Martini, Jr.

DOO-DOO .... Bill Phillips

CARMINE .... Jeff Robins

EDIE KEATON .... Andrea Maulella

MICHELE .... Liz Zazzi

CHARACTERS

VINCENT DIDONATO – 46, unattached, and unevolved. "Marty" as played by "Ralph Kramden." Would like to find love but feels as if all his efforts will come to naught.

DOO-DOO – 45, shop foreman, Vinnie's oldest friend, sees himself as an idea man. Ed Norton to Vincent's Ralph Cramden.

CARMINE – 45, a welder. Emotional. He is always crying or on the verge of tears.

EDIE KEATON – 38, a down-on-her-luck actress/waitress trying to return to the business after a difficult divorce. Sure of herself onstage. Offstage, not so much. Has a heart of gold but has been burned one too many times.

MICHELE – 38, Edie's best friend and protector. An artist, tough as nails.

SETTING

New York City

TIME

1999, just before the world changed

AUTHORS' NOTES

The acting style in *Centennial Casting* should be broad and farcical...it's really *The Honeymooners* with a big heart. And like *The Honeymooners*, there are moments of pathos where the actors can slow down and reveal themselves.

This play is for Danny and Andrew.

ACT ONE

Scene One – The Office

(The office of Centennial Casting. It is drab and rundown, the walls are covered with papers and notes that are yellowed and out of print. A picture of John F. Kennedy adorns one wall next to a huge Frank Sinatra button that reads, "It's Sinatra's World, we just live in it." The office has the feel of an ancient filing system that made sense to only one person and that person is not coming back.)

(VINCENT DIDONATO *stands behind the desk, frantically talking on the phone. He is overwhelmed by the office, the paperwork, his mother's absence. It's ten a.m. and he wants a sandwich. He's talking, filing, and searching for something at the same time...poorly.)*

VINCENT. No, I'm sorry, that's not the kind of thing we do. We generally cast with ceramic back, sometimes epoxy and...no, we don't do precision work anymore – Hello? Hello? What is it with this phone?

(He hangs up, the phone rings again.)

(Answers phone.) Centennial Casting. *(No?)* Oh, Hi Mike. I'm sorry, I'm still looking for this thing. No, no I know it's here somewhere. It's just that the shop's a mess right now and – yeah, thank you. I appreciate that. Seventy-six years old. I know, she kept books for my grandfather for chrissakes. That's why nobody knows where the hell anything is. Hey, that's the way

it goes. One day you're cooking tripe, and the next day you're dead. Hold on a sec. *(He calls to the door.)* DOO-DOO! Hang on a second Mikey. DOO-DOO! Get in here, willya?

> *(**DOO-DOO** pokes his head through the door; he's a bit overwhelmed as well.)*

DOO-DOO. You want coffee?

VINCENT. Help me find this frigging PO.

> *(He hands **DOO-DOO** a slip of paper, then into the phone:)*

Hang on Mikey.

*(To **DOO-DOO**.)* Where did my mother keep this stuff?

DOO-DOO. On the board.

VINCENT. What?

DOO-DOO. On the board, strunad.

> *(He moves to a folder stuffed in a crevice.)*

Here, what is it, 9-1, there it is, right there.

> *(He quickly hands it to **VINCENT**.)*

VINCENT. That's it. Oh, that's it. Thanks. Mikey. Mikey? This phone! He hung up.

DOO-DOO. He'll call back. You want coffee?

VINCENT. No. This office is a mess.

DOO-DOO. It's always been like this.

VINCENT. How the hell did she find anything?

DOO-DOO. I don't know, she knew where everything was.

VINCENT. But nothing's labeled, look at this. Boxes everywhere –

DOO-DOO. Hey, if you poked your head out of the plating room once in a while, maybe you'd know what was going on around here.

VINCENT. That's just it, I didn't wanna know. I never wanted to run this joint.

DOO-DOO. You had to figure you would someday.

VINCENT. No, I figured Mom would retire and we'd sell the place.

DOO-DOO. Well. She never got her chance.

VINCENT. Look at this. Shoeboxes full of stuff. Like you found that PO. What the hell was it doing there?

DOO-DOO. There's a pieca cardboard, see? Look on the bulletin board. "Mikey Triano's POs."

VINCENT. But why isn't it in the file cabinet?

DOO-DOO. 'Cause she knows that Mikey always loses stuff on his end, so he's gonna be calling for some kinda information from you and rather than file it away, she puts it up on the bulletin board where she can find it quick. And since she knows that the first thing you're gonna do is look on the bulletin board, there's other notes on the board telling you where to find other stuff. Here, look at this. "Orders for Femic are in the bottom drawer in the back." And this one. "Chase Welding is now Eliott Welding. The Eliott Welding Files are where the Chase Welding Files used to be."

VINCENT. So where's the Chase Welding File?

DOO-DOO. Nowhere, they went outta business.

And here's another one, "Make sure –" oh forget it.

VINCENT. What?

DOO-DOO. Nothing, I'm getting coffee. The Ptomaine Truck will be here any minute.

VINCENT. *(Going to the same spot and reading.)* "Make sure you order the cake for Vincent's birthday."

DOO-DOO. She was gonna surprise you.

VINCENT. Oh.

(Knock at the door.)

CARMINE. Hey boss, it's Carmine!

*(**VINCENT** and **CARMINE** look at each other.)*

VINCENT. Come on in Carmine!

(**CARMINE** *enters, holding a bouquet of flowers. He is lanky with a sad face. He is always crying or on the verge of tears.*)

CARMINE. Hey boss?

VINCENT. What's this?

CARMINE. It's a Pick-Me-Up Bouquet from Oakdale across the street.

DOO-DOO. That was nice.

CARMINE. Where do you want me to put 'em?

VINCENT. Put it with the others, in the back.

CARMINE. It's a lovely arrangement.

VINCENT. Yeah. You okay?

CARMINE. This is tough you know?

VINCENT. I know what you mean.

CARMINE. I couldn't sleep last night. Or the night before.

VINCENT. Aaayy, Carmine...

CARMINE. She was like a mother to me.

DOO-DOO. You got a mother. You live with your mother.

CARMINE. She was like a mother to my mother!

DOO-DOO. Get outta here, you mother.

CARMINE. I'm sorry Vinnie, this is just –

VINCENT. I know, I know.

CARMINE. I mean, if you ever wanna talk –

VINCENT. Yeah, thanks. I appreciate –

CARMINE. – I'm there for you.

(*He sniffles and exits.* **DOO-DOO** *and* **VINCENT** *watch him go.*)

DOO-DOO. We now return to our regularly scheduled program.

(*Pause.*)

So, mister birthday boy, what are you doing on the big day?

VINCENT. What I always do. Go to OTB.

DOO-DOO. You cannot spend your birthday at Off Track Betting.

VINCENT. I can and I will.

DOO-DOO. Oh come on.

VINCENT. Hey, who knows, maybe I'll pick a winner for once.

DOO-DOO. You wanna go to the ballgame or something?

VINCENT. Nah.

DOO-DOO. How's about you and me, we meet Suzette and her cousin for a beer? This cousin, Vinnie, she's not half bad. Owns her own dog grooming salon.

VINCENT. Thanks, Cujo, I think I'll pass.

DOO-DOO. Come on, Vinnie.

VINCENT. Doo-Doo, I told you, I'm not interested in any more of your matchmaking. What was the last disaster? The masseuse with the lazy eye?

DOO-DOO. Vinnie, that was two years ago.

VINCENT. I'm just starting to get feeling back in my tuchus.

DOO-DOO. You gotta get out, live a little.

VINCENT. Forget it.

> (*He sits behind the desk.*)

DOO-DOO. You know, ever since Carolyn left, it's like you crawled under a rock.

VINCENT. Don't start.

DOO-DOO. All right. All right.

> (*He begins to leave.*)

VINCENT. Wait, who's this?

DOO-DOO. What?

VINCENT. The girl.

> (**VINCENT** *holds up an eight-by-ten picture and résumé.*)

DOO-DOO. Oh, we get some of those now and then.

VINCENT. Who is she?

DOO-DOO. It's a, whatdoyoucallit, actress. Look, there's a whole stash of 'em, see?

> *(He reaches underneath the in-box and pulls out a short stack of pictures and résumés.)*

These people, they send 'em out, I guess, and they think this is one of them casting agent places. They must see it in the phone book or something so they drop off their pictures.

VINCENT. You're kidding. How long has this been happening?

DOO-DOO. I don't know. Comes in spurts, we used to get like one a week. Your mother loved 'em. Read the back, there's funny stuff on there.

VINCENT. *(Reading.)* "Good with children and animals."

DOO-DOO. Right? I'm good with 'em too, somebody gonna make a movie about me?

VINCENT. "Drives stick and automatic." That's an acting skill?

DOO-DOO. Oh yeah. They gotta drive cars sometimes. Like in chase scenes.

VINCENT. They get stunt people to do that. Why the hell's she gotta say she drives a car? Hey, this one can cook.

DOO-DOO. Where?

VINCENT. Right here. Gourmet cook. Hey, not bad, she can juggle, deal blackjack –

DOO-DOO. At the same time?

VINCENT. Doesn't say. Ballroom dancing. That's nice. *(Reading.)* Look at this one. Handicaps horses.

DOO-DOO. Get out.

VINCENT. Right there. Handicaps horses.

DOO-DOO. Hey, that's a chick for you.

VINCENT. I never seen anybody at OTB who looked like this.

DOO-DOO. *(Grabbing the box of photos.)* I gotta get back to work. You want me to dump these?

VINCENT. Yeah, go ahead. This place is so piled with shit I can't find my – wait a minute. Let me see that one again.

(**DOO-DOO** *hands* **VINCENT** *the photo.*)

You know, she looks familiar.

DOO-DOO. Maybe from the TV.

VINCENT. Aaaayyy, she was a juror on *Law and Order*.

DOO-DOO. Which *Law and Order*? Every other show is *Law and Order*. They got *Law and Order SUV*, one, two, three, M-O-U-S-E...Madonn, who thinks up this shit?

VINCENT. Doesn't say which one.

DOO-DOO. Pretty girl.

VINCENT. You ain't kidding. Edie Keaton. Can't place her...

DOO-DOO. So why don't you call her, Mr. Studley?

VINCENT. Get back to work.

(**VINCENT** *hands* **DOO-DOO** *the résumé.*)

DOO-DOO. You should give her a call, her number's right –

VINCENT. I don't have time for this shit.

DOO-DOO. All right, I'm getting coffee. You don't want nothing?

VINCENT. No.

DOO-DOO. Piece of fruit?

VINCENT. No.

DOO-DOO. Yogurt?

(**VINCENT** *gives him a look of contempt.*)

VINCENT. No.

DOO-DOO. A cruller.

VINCENT. Make it two.

DOO-DOO. You'll be here?

VINCENT. Yeah, I'll be here.

(**DOO-DOO** *exits.*)

Where else am I gonna be?

(*Blackout.*)

Scene Two

(In the darkness, we hear the beep of a phone machine and a woman's voice; she seems incompetent, even at this simple task.)

EDIE. *(Voice-over.)* Hi, this is Edie. Leave me a message and I'll get back to you soon. You have about a minute. Not counting what I just said. I think. Or, a little of what I just said. I'm sorry. I'm taking up your time. Okay. Start now. At the beep.

(We hear a beep.)

DOO-DOO. *(Voice-over.)* Hello, Miss Keaton. I'm calling for Mr. Vincent DiDonato at Centennial Casting, 212-555-5574. We received your picture and we'd like to talk to you so give me a call, give him a call Vincent, that's Vincent D-I-D-O-N-A-T-O sometime tomorrow, like maybe 12:30 because that's when he's at his desk eating something. Thank you and I hope your day is a pleasant day.

Scene Three – The Diner

(The Moondance Diner. **EDIE** *stands at the counter talking to* **MICHELE**, *who holds a pot of coffee and a check. They both are staring at* **EDIE***'s cell phone quizzically.)*

EDIE. I think I deleted it.

MICHELE. Cursor up.

EDIE. What cursor?

MICHELE. Cursor, cursor. The arrow. No, up!

EDIE. All right.

MICHELE. Give me the phone. I'll find the number.

EDIE. Seven wants their check.

MICHELE. I gave you their check.

EDIE. I thought it was for six.

MICHELE. No, check for seven, coffee for six. Here's the number, call.

EDIE. Wait.

*(**MICHELE** takes the coffee pot and exits. **EDIE** begins to steel herself to make the phone call.)*

Okay. Here we go. Gonna dial. "Hello, this is Edie Keaton." "Hello" –

*(**MICHELE** returns.)*

MICHELE. Did you get it?

EDIE. Yeah, I'm calling right now.

MICHELE. Take your time, I'll watch your station.

EDIE. Wait.

MICHELE. What?

EDIE. Don't go, stay with me.

MICHELE. I gotta take an order, you got four covers on three.

EDIE. I need you to stay with me.

MICHELE. Why?

EDIE. Because when I have to do these things, I freeze up.

MICHELE. You freeze up when you have to make a phone call.

EDIE. Yes.

MICHELE. Since when?

EDIE. It's not with everyone. It's only industry people.

MICHELE. Oh please.

EDIE. It's true. Drake says I have a blockage.

MICHELE. Drake...

EDIE. My life coach.

MICHELE. Oh, right.

EDIE. He says, "I need to put myself in a position to succeed but I can't find that position as long as there's blockage." See, we have these strategies for success and it all makes sense when I'm in the room talking to him. But then, when I'm by myself, it's like, poof, where'd that go?

MICHELE. Why don't you get Drake the Wonder Boy to be in the room with you?

EDIE. I can't. He fired me.

MICHELE. Your life coach fired you?

EDIE. Yes. This morning.

MICHELE. Why?

EDIE. He said he couldn't fix my life.

MICHELE. What?

EDIE. He said he was sorry, but I was beyond his reach.

MICHELE. Did he refer you to someone?

EDIE. No. He said he didn't know anyone who was right for my particular blockage.

MICHELE. You know what, you should have told that new age nutjob to take that crystal of his and stick it up his –

EDIE. No, I just told him I was sorry.

MICHELE. Edie, your life coach doesn't fire you, you're supposed to fire him!

EDIE. Just stand here for a minute. If you're with me, I bet I can do it.

MICHELE. No. I'm gonna go take care of an order. And while I'm doing that, you're gonna talk to the casting guy.

EDIE. No.

MICHELE. Yes.

EDIE. I can't do it by myself. I might throw up or speak in tongues. I should just quit.

MICHELE. You can't quit, I can't cover lunch alone.

EDIE. I don't mean this. I mean, New York. I mean acting.

MICHELE. Yeah, yeah, make the call.

EDIE. I didn't want to say anything, but they called, the school in Ohio where I was substituting called and they wanted to know if I would take over the drama club. It's part-time, but it would have benefits and...

MICHELE. You aren't going anywhere. Give me the phone.

EDIE. I think I could even get dental. I've never had dental.

MICHELE. Give me the phone.

EDIE. Why?

MICHELE. Give it to me!

(**EDIE** *hands* **MICHELE** *the phone.*)

What's that thing that you and Drake did when you're not supposed to talk?

When you're only supposed to listen and not say anything?

EDIE. Oh, glass booth.

MICHELE. Right. Glass booth. You're in the glass booth.

EDIE. No way, I'm not in the –

MICHELE. Glass booth!

EDIE. But –

MICHELE. You get in that booth! I'm gonna talk, you're gonna listen. And when I'm done talking you're gonna get out of the booth and call the guy. Get it? Just nod.

(**EDIE** *purses her lips and nods.*)

Edie, you've been my best friend since fourth grade and I love you like a sister. And I know how you feel, I really do. But I'm not gonna let you quit! Hey, I'm an artist too. Don't you think there are days when I feel like giving up? I got those two cast iron dragonflies I've been working on. I've been working on that damn sculpture forever and it keeps falling apart. And if it ain't done in six weeks, I'm gonna lose the commission. But you don't see me giving up. You know why? 'Cause nobody likes a quitter. Not to mention I gotta set a good example for my kid.

EDIE. You're a great mom, Mish – (**MICHELE** *stops her.*)

MICHELE. Glass booth!! But, you, Edie, I gotta say, you find ways to screw things up that defy the imagination. Every audition turns into an adventure! You go to the wrong location. You show up on the wrong day. If you go on the right day, you show up at the wrong time. Then the one time you do get to an audition you get all nutsy kookoo.

EDIE. Can I come out of the booth?

MICHELE. For a second.

EDIE. That's not true.

MICHELE. What happened the last time you had an audition?

EDIE. Oh, the spot for the yeast infection cream?

MICHELE. Yeah. You told me when you auditioned you did some kind of...what was it, interpretive dance while scratching yourself?

EDIE. I thought it was right for the character.

MICHELE. What character? It's some chick with a yeast infection. Just smile and ride the stupid stationary bike like they asked you to!

EDIE. It's the damn audition, Mish. I just can't do it. Once I get the job, I'm fine, I'm wonderful. It's just the audition, I freeze up, I screw up, terrible things happen!!

MICHELE. Don't start...

EDIE. You know it's true, I'm cursed! I'm cursed, ever since that damned audition at the Folger!

MICHELE. Enough with the curse. That could have happened to anyone! Edie, listen to me. You're a wonderful actress. So no matter how many times you screw up, I will not let you quit.

EDIE. Why?

MICHELE. When my ex-husband tried to kill me with a snow shovel, who let me live on their couch with my kid for eight months?

EDIE. That was very nice of me.

MICHELE. It was. You didn't quit on me. And I'm not gonna let you quit on you. Because one of these days, Edie, you're gonna get it right. Get ready to start talking.

> (**EDIE** *begins dialing.*)

EDIE. I'm not talking, I'm still in the booth!

MICHELE. Here we go –

EDIE. Wait, don't hit send.

MICHELE. Get out of that booth!

EDIE. In a minute.

MICHELE. What?

EDIE. I gotta do something...okay. *(Takes a deep breath and repeats a mantra to herself.)* "I am focused, I am fearless. I am focused, I am fearless."

MICHELE. You are focused, you are fearless and you're fucked if you don't make that call right now!

EDIE. Okay, hit it.

> (**MICHELE** *hits send, hands* **EDIE** *the phone, grabs the coffee pot, and exits.*)

MICHELE. Good luck, kid.

> (**EDIE** *holds the phone up to her face in fear.*)
> (*Blackout.*)

Scene Four – The Office

*(Back at the office, a few days later. **VINCENT** is sitting at his desk. **DOO-DOO** wears a party hat and holds a blower. **CARMINE** also wears a party hat but, as usual, he is holding back tears. **VINCENT**'s hat is on his desk.)*

DOO-DOO. Put on the hat.

VINCENT. I don't want to put on the hat.

DOO-DOO. It's your birthday.

*(**DOO-DOO** puts the hat on **VINCENT**'s head.)*

VINCENT. I appreciate this, but –

DOO-DOO. This is a special day. How often do you turn fifty?

VINCENT. What fifty, I'm forty-seven...

DOO-DOO. I thought you were turning fifty.

VINCENT. You thought wrong.

DOO-DOO. Shit, you look terrible. What was all that with your mother crying all the time, my Vincent, he'll be fifty and he'll be all alone?

VINCENT. She was thinking ahead.

DOO-DOO. All right, forty-seven...you wanna go first Carmine?

CARMINE. Yeah.

*(He hands a present to **VINCENT**.)*

This is for you.

VINCENT. Carmine. You shouldn't have.

CARMINE. It's just a little something.

*(**VINCENT** opens the package to reveal a picture frame.)*

VINCENT. It's a picture of you. And my mother.

CARMINE. I thought you'd like to have it.

VINCENT. This is very...it's very nice.

CARMINE. Thanks. She meant a lot to me.

VINCENT. Yeah. I know.

CARMINE. I just thought that...

(*Overcome,* **CARMINE** *exits.*)

VINCENT. There's a movie in that guy's head that nobody else has got a ticket to.

DOO-DOO. Here, open mine.

VINCENT. What do you got there, lottery tickets?

DOO-DOO. Nah, not this year. It's not a present exactly, more like a card...

(*He hands* **VINCENT** *the card.*)

Many happy returns.

VINCENT. Doo-Doo, what did you do this for?

DOO-DOO. Every year on my birthday your ma gave me a bottle of Asti. Used to pop it open and have a drink with me, right here at this desk. It's the least I could do.

VINCENT. (*Reading card.*) "Fifty is Nifty."

(*He gives* **DOO-DOO** *a look.*)

DOO-DOO. You're supposed to sing this part.

VINCENT.

"HAPPY BIRTHDAY TO YOU
A GIRL WILL CALL YOU
RIGHT AFTER YOUR LUNCH BREAK
SO THEN YOU CAN SCREW."

A girl, what girl?

DOO-DOO. I got this girl to call you, as a birthday present.

VINCENT. What are you talking, like a stripper?

DOO-DOO. Nah, the actress, Edie what's her face. I noticed you still have her picture on your desk.

VINCENT. Yeah, so...?

DOO-DOO. So I left her a message on her machine, telling her I was from the Centennial Casting Agency and you wanted to talk to her and she should call you today around 12:30 and I thought maybe you could talk to her and you know, ask her out to dinner or something. So happy birthday.

VINCENT. Are you shitting me?

DOO-DOO. No, you like it?

VINCENT. Doo-Doo I'm gonna kill you!

DOO-DOO. Don't you wanna meet her?

VINCENT. Of course, but –

DOO-DOO. So now you get to meet her.

VINCENT. But I don't want to meet her like this. Besides, she ain't gonna be interested in me.

DOO-DOO. Of course she will.

VINCENT. This is a sophisticated lady. What are we gonna talk about? Life in the plating room?

DOO-DOO. No, no. You talk about the theatre. You pretend you're some casting guy. How hard can that be? You say you're making a movie, you tell her you'll put her on *All My Children* or some shit like that. My nephew, Joseph, I was talking to him about this...

VINCENT. What the hell does he know?

DOO-DOO. He was in a movie. With Spike Lee. He was the white guy hanging out in a bar. You shoulda seen him, he was pretty good.

VINCENT. Doo-Doo, you're completely whacked.

DOO-DOO. He said, and I wrote this down, to tell this girl to come in for a "general." A general, that's like to try out for a part, when you don't know what the part is. To like see what they can do.

VINCENT. I'm not doing that.

DOO-DOO. And then when she's here you just give her some acting lines and sit there and look interested and then ask her if she wants to go eat something. Great idea, right?

    (The phone rings.)

That must be the young lady now.

VINCENT. Jesus Christ –

DOO-DOO. Centennial Casting? How may I help you?

VINCENT. *(Panicked.)* I'm not here!

DOO-DOO. Mr. DiDonato is right here. May I ask who is calling?

VINCENT. Jesus.

DOO-DOO. Edie Keaton. One moment please.

> *(Handing* **VINCENT** *the phone.)*

It's for you.

VINCENT. *(Panics further, not knowing what to say.)* Hello? Yes, this is Vincent DiDonato, what can I do for you? Who? Oh yeah, yeah. Miss Keaton.

> *(He gives* **DOO-DOO** *a look.)*

Yeah, look, I'm sorry, lady, but there's been some mistake. We're not, we're not seeing any more actresses, today. We're full up with actresses this month. You understand? I'm very sorry but –

> *(Pause.)*

Yeah, I know –

> *(Pause.)*

Okay, Miss Keaton? Miss Keaton? Now what do you got to go and do that for?

> *(He winces, as he can't stand hearing a woman cry.)*

Miss Keaton? Hey, Edie! Your name is Edie, right? I know, I know, it's just...hey, hey, blow your nose or something, I'll...look, I'll squeeze you in. All right? Okay? I said, "I'll squeeze you in." Come by...how does tomorrow sound? Two o'clock? Okay? Okay, just stop crying, for Christ's sake. Where? Uh...

> *(***DOO-DOO** *motions "here.")*

Here. I mean, in the uh...casting office here at 254 Houston. You'll see the sign on the door. Yeah, yeah, you're welcome, you're welcome. You okay now? Then see ya tomorrow. At two.

> *(He hangs up.)*

VINCENT. I'M GOING TO HAVE YOUR BALLS LAMINATED!

DOO-DOO. Hey, you were great!

VINCENT. What do I do once she gets here?

DOO-DOO. Don't worry, I got it all figured out.

VINCENT. I was trying to tell her the truth, but the chick started bawling.

DOO-DOO. But you're like a natural. You knew the lingo and everything.

VINCENT. What lingo?

DOO-DOO. "I'll squeeze you in." That was good. Here, take this.

(He sticks a cigar in **VINCENT**'s *mouth.)*

Vincent DiDonato, casting agent to the stars!

(Blackout.)

Scene Five – The Office

(The casting office has been transformed to look like a real casting office. **VINCENT** *and* **DOO-DOO** *are frantically taping the headshots onto the wall behind the desk. Things have been swept and all the machine parts and girlie calendars have been removed.)*

DOO-DOO. All right, let's go through it again, she walks through the door and you say what.

VINCENT. How do you do, *(Puts his hand out.)* I'm Vincent DiDonato –

DOO-DOO. Don't shake.

VINCENT. I gotta shake.

DOO-DOO. Them people never shake. They're like standoffish, you know?

VINCENT. All right, I don't shake. What do I do, wave?

DOO-DOO. You nod. Like this. *(He demonstrates.)*

VINCENT. Meaning what?

DOO-DOO. It means like I know you're here and I'm gonna see if you've got what it takes.

VINCENT. I don't mean that.

DOO-DOO. Course you do.

VINCENT. Look, I just wanna get this over with.

DOO-DOO. You gotta make like you're a casting person. Now do it again, with the nod.

VINCENT. How do I do – I mean, how do you do, I'm Vincent DiDonato of Centennial Casting.

DOO-DOO. You ain't gotta say the casting part.

VINCENT. Why not?

DOO-DOO. The name is right on the door, the chick can read.

VINCENT. All right, so then what?

DOO-DOO. You make small talk. What's it like out there, has it stopped raining yet –

VINCENT. It ain't raining.

DOO-DOO. So you say, "Does it look like it's gonna start raining."

VINCENT. *(Overlapping.)* She ain't auditioning for the fucking weather girl.

DOO-DOO. Forget it – you ain't gotta say nothing. Once she's in the door, all you gotta do is sit down and check her out, see?

VINCENT. I don't know.

DOO-DOO. Come on, it's just like a first date.

VINCENT. I ain't been on a first date in years.

DOO-DOO. You ain't been on *any* date in years. This is gonna be a pieca cake. My nephew was telling me all about it. You just sit like this.

> *(He gets behind the desk and crosses one hand over the other.)*

And then you say, "So tell me about yourself." And she's gonna start talking. Every now and then, you smile, you nod. But you ain't gotta say nothing. You just have to make like, "Oh, is that so. That's interesting. You don't say? I've thought that many times myself." If she says something funny you laugh, but not too much. Just make like you're interested, but not *that* interested. Capisce?

VINCENT. Okay.

DOO-DOO. And then you say...

VINCENT. So what are you going to do for us today?

DOO-DOO. Good! And then she does it.

VINCENT. What do I say when she's done?

DOO-DOO. Nothing. You say, "Thank you."

VINCENT. And that's it.

DOO-DOO. That's it. She leaves.

VINCENT. Doo, this ain't gonna work.

DOO-DOO. Have fun with it.

VINCENT. I'm no good at meeting women. I never know what to say.

DOO-DOO. That's the beauty of it. You don't have to say nothing, she's gonna do all the talking. Remember, *she's* trying to impress *you.*

VINCENT. I just don't wanna screw this up.

DOO-DOO. You won't.

VINCENT. I screwed things up with Carolyn.

DOO-DOO. Don't start, Vinnie –

VINCENT. No matter what I did, I could never make her happy.

DOO-DOO. Here we go –

VINCENT. Best eleven years of my life and I blew it. Maybe I don't know how to be in a relationship. Maybe I'm not giving enough.

DOO-DOO. *(Overlapping "Maybe I'm not giving enough.")* Vinnie…

VINCENT. That's what Carolyn was always telling me.

DOO-DOO. What did she know? She left you for the cable guy! Come on Vinnie…gimme the smile.

VINCENT. What smile?

DOO-DOO. The Vincent DiDonato "I ain't got no money but I got a whole lotta love" smile. Come on baby!

> *(**VINCENT** smiles.)*

There it is.

> *(There is a knock at the door.)*

That's our girl.

VINCENT. Wait. What do I say at the end?

DOO-DOO. You say, "Thanks for coming in."

VINCENT. Thanks for coming in.

DOO-DOO. Right. Answer the door.

VINCENT. *(Rehearsing.)* Thanks for coming in.

DOO-DOO. Come on, she's waiting.

VINCENT. Where you gonna be?

DOO-DOO. I'm gonna go on the shop floor and make sure those jamokes keep quiet.

VINCENT. Wait, I can't breathe.

DOO-DOO. Answer the door.

VINCENT. This is the most screwed-up thing –

DOO-DOO. Go answer the door!

VINCENT. All right!

> (**DOO-DOO** *exits onto the shop floor.* **VINCENT**
> *begins rehearsing.*)

Thanks for coming in.

> (**VINCENT** *speaks to the framed picture of his
> mother on the wall. He straightens his hair
> in the glass and then goes to answer the door.*)

Thanks for coming in.

EDIE. Hello.

VINCENT. Thanks for coming in.

EDIE. Hi, I'm Kedie Eaton. I mean, Edie Keaton.

> (**VINCENT** *is immediately taken by her.*)

VINCENT. Thanks for coming in.

EDIE. Hello Mr. DiDonato.

VINCENT. Yes, yes. Call me Vincent.

EDIE. Hi Vincent.

VINCENT. Thanks for coming in.

EDIE. First of all, I am so sorry I cried on the phone –

VINCENT. Oh that's –

EDIE. – Yesterday. I was having such a bad –

VINCENT. I know.

EDIE. – Day, and usually it doesn't get to me –

VINCENT. Of course.

EDIE. – But it was just one of those moments when –

VINCENT. Sure.

EDIE. – Everything just...poof! You know?

VINCENT. Boom!

EDIE. Just like that.

VINCENT. Just blows up in your face.

EDIE. Right. I hope you don't mind I'm early.

VINCENT. Not at all.

EDIE. 'Cause I'm late a lot of the time and I wanted to make sure this time that I got here on time and I guess I don't know my own strength. I mean I didn't know how early I could be. When I try to be...early.

VINCENT. *(Smiles. Pause.)* Thanks for coming in.

EDIE. Thanks for having me.

VINCENT. Let me take your sweater off. I mean you can take your sweater off. If you want to. If you need to. You can do what you like.

EDIE. Oh, that's all right. It's a little chilly.

VINCENT. It is. It is chilly. Yes. Brrrrr. We're going through some renovations and we're actually in the process of moving because down here it's getting to be too much, the cold. I mean, not that other parts of the city are warmer. But the heat here is, I mean, jeez it's god awful. Too hot in the winter and way too cold in the summer. I mean, well, the other way around actually. Too cold in the summer and way too...hot...you know this place just don't work so good.

EDIE. I see.

VINCENT. Did you have trouble finding it?

EDIE. No, not at all.

VINCENT. 'Cause it's in kind of an out of the way area away from the other, casting agents, agencies...offices, on the row there. The theatre row. Where the other offices are.

EDIE. Things are kind of spread all over these days.

VINCENT. Yes, they certainly are. Spread all over the place. Things are changing and that usually means spreading. I mean changing – so tell me about yourself.

> *(At the last second, **VINCENT** remembers he's supposed to be sitting behind the desk. He rushes behind the desk, trying to replay the moment.)*

So tell me about yourself.

(He then suddenly folds his hands, as Doo-Doo instructed.)

EDIE. Well – wait. Ham and cheese, whiskey down!

VINCENT. Yeah, that's...that's my sandwich. How did you –

EDIE. I work at the Moondance Diner! Last summer – I was thinking to myself, where do I know him from – you used to come in all the time.

VINCENT. How do you like that?

EDIE. Now I know. You were working on that film, right? Casting that film with Morgan Freeman, right?

VINCENT. Yes! Morgan Friedman!

EDIE. They were shooting in the warehouse near the river. I didn't know you were casting that.

VINCENT. Oh yes –

EDIE. *Melody of Fear.*

VINCENT. That's it.

EDIE. No!

VINCENT. No!

EDIE. That was the summer before.

VINCENT. The summer before!

EDIE. What was the name of it?

VINCENT. I'm drawing a blank.

*(All of a sudden **CARMINE** enters, crying.)*

CARMINE. Vinnie...

VINCENT. Oh, uh, excuse me –

CARMINE. I'm sorry to interrupt...

EDIE. No problem –

VINCENT. What the hell are you doing?

CARMINE. I'm sorry! I've just been thinking about your mother and all that we went through together and it's just so overwhelming. I know, now is not the time, but –

VINCENT. No, that's good, Carmine. That's real good.

(VINCENT puts his arm around CARMINE and guides him back toward the door.)

You're really starting to get the emotional...what do you call it...range of the character. There. So why don't you go back on the shop...acting...area there and keep working on it. Okay?

CARMINE. Okay, but –

VINCENT. All right, nice work.

(VINCENT slams the door shut.)

Sorry about that.

EDIE. Who was that?

VINCENT. That? That there was Carmine, one of my clients, my actor clients, there. We're trying to find the right project for him. Very talented. Very, very talented, that Carmine.

EDIE. There's an intensity about him.

VINCENT. There is. That. But never mind him, let's talk about you. Edie.

EDIE. Well, I brought you a résumé.

VINCENT. I already got one. Let's see here...

(He fumbles through a pile and picks out **EDIE.***)*

That's you, right?

EDIE. Oh wow, that's an old one.

VINCENT. Well, I was gonna say, you do look different. Better, but different.

EDIE. I haven't sent those out for three years, at least.

VINCENT. Oh. Well, it spoke to me, this picture. Periodically, what we do in the office, if uh...if we're in a period where we want to do a lot of auditioning generally, I mean, general auditioning, general auditions, the general thing, we'll look through the files and clean them out a bit and see what's what. And your file, your résumé just came to the top and uh, well –

EDIE. Here I am.

VINCENT. Very becoming. Looks just like you. Which of course it should.

EDIE. *(Looks at the new and old pictures.)* Wow, I've gotten a little older, huh?

VINCENT. Nah, not really. How much aging can you do in three years.

EDIE. I got married three years ago. You can age quite a bit.

VINCENT. Oh, you're married?

EDIE. Divorced.

VINCENT. Oh, that's good. I mean, not good. But...you know what I mean. If it was a good thing for you to be divorced, then it's good that you are.

EDIE. It's okay, I know what you mean...

VINCENT. You do? That's good. 'Cause sometimes, I don't even know what the hell it is I'm talking about. So tell me about yourself.

EDIE. Well, I'm originally from Freehold, New Jersey. I've kind of been out of the business for, well, the past three years. When I got married, I was gonna stop acting for a while, I moved to Ohio with my husband. My ex-husband. He was supposed to have a great job out there, but that didn't work out, the job, or the being married to him, so...

VINCENT. So you're back.

EDIE. I'm back. I've done some showcases around the city and I did some soap work too. I had an under-five, it's down there, I was on *Guiding Light.*

VINCENT. Really?

EDIE. Yeah. Do you watch the show?

VINCENT. Now and then, it was my mother's favorite show –

EDIE. 'Cause do you remember last year when Frankie was getting married to the guy over from Cyprus.

VINCENT. Of course, who could forget?

EDIE. Well remember how they had to bring the whole family over from the islands and Frankie's grandmother had a dream that the marriage would be cursed unless she was married in the presence of the sacred statue from the square of the village in Cyprus? And she wouldn't give her blessings unless they flew in the statue, so then Frankie got the idea that they could replicate the statue and trick the grandmother?

VINCENT. You were the statue?

EDIE. No, I was the woman who *unveiled* the statue.

VINCENT. Really?

EDIE. It wasn't just unveiling it, I had a couple of lines and some very nice business too.

VINCENT. That's great. Good for you.

EDIE. Thanks.

VINCENT. Sure.

EDIE. And of course, getting back into it and everything, I feel like I'm like starting over, you know? Which is tough, very tough. Very, very, very tough, but I'm determined, I'm going to strive for success and give birth to my life plan...

VINCENT. Well, it's –

EDIE. I think that's why I was crying on the phone, 'cause I kinda felt like everybody forgot me and then I get a call to meet you and I know it's nothing. I mean, not that it's nothing, nothing. But it's just good to get out there and audition again, you know?

VINCENT. Sure.

EDIE. You gotta wait out these valleys, right?

VINCENT. Yeah, 'cause sometimes it feels like nothing is happening and then somebody walks through the door and you're feeling all sorts of um...newness.

(*Pause.*)

So, what are you gonna be doing for us today? I mean, me. Today.

EDIE. Well, I thought I'd do something from *(Whispers.)* *The Scottish Play.*

VINCENT. *(Whispers, unsure of what she's talking about.)* Excellent choice.

EDIE. *(Stops whispering.)* Is that okay? I know people usually want to see something more contemporary, but Shakespeare is my first love. That's really my dream.

VINCENT. To act in Shakespeare.

EDIE. Oh sure. Absolutely. I mean, what could be better?

VINCENT. You got me.

EDIE. So that's what I'm gonna do for you today. Lady Macbeth. If that's all right.

VINCENT. Go right ahead.

EDIE. Okay.

> (**EDIE** *smiles and stands behind the chair, prepping herself. She is very nervous and throughout the audition continues to hold her purse, as if ready to run.* **VINCENT** *pours himself a cup of water.)*

"What beast was't then that made you break this enterprise to me?
When you durst do it, *then* you were a man;
And, to be more than what you were, you would
Be so much more the man. Nor time nor place
Did then adhere, and yet you would make both:
They have made themselves, and that their fitness now
Does unmake you. I have given suck –"

> *(On the word "suck,"* **VINCENT** *does a spit-take and begins to cough.* **EDIE** *stops.)*

Oh my god, are you okay?

VINCENT. I'm fine keep – *(He coughs some more, tries to clear his throat.)* – going –

EDIE. Are you sure?

VINCENT. Yes, yes. I'm good. Don't stop.

EDIE. Put your arms up over your head!!

VINCENT. Huh?

EDIE. Your arms!! Up over your head!!!

VINCENT. *(Raises his arms.)* I'm fine...

EDIE. Are you sure?

VINCENT. I'm sure. Really. Can I put my arms down?

> *(She nods, terrified. He puts his arms down.)*

EDIE. Yes.

> *(She grabs her coat and rushes to the door.)*

VINCENT. What are you –

EDIE. I'm sorry. Listen, I'm just – I don't think I'm ready to –

VINCENT. Where you going?

EDIE. This isn't going to work. I appreciate you having me in, but I'm just not ready to be out auditioning...

VINCENT. Edie –

EDIE. I need to spend more time in class and – I mean, I need to find a class and then spend more time in it and...

VINCENT. Edie, I thought you were great.

EDIE. Really?

VINCENT. Absolutely. You had a...quality.

EDIE. Yeah?

VINCENT. It was shimmering. Like a star.

EDIE. Oh. Oh, well, thank you.

> *(Pause.)*

Mr. DiDonato?

VINCENT. Vincent.

EDIE. Vincent, can I ask you a question?

VINCENT. Go ahead.

EDIE. *(Looking around the office suspiciously.)* Well, if you don't mind me asking, what kind of things do you cast out of this office?

VINCENT. Oh, we run the gauntlet. A lot of things. Movies, television programs, theatrical events, uh...movies...

I'm sure we have lots that you would be right for. This being a general of course, I just wanted to see what you could do –

EDIE. Of course. What are you casting now?

VINCENT. Uh, now, I'm casting a...uh...you know, it's still in the works. I'm not supposed to say anything. We're just dotting the t's and crossing the i's, I mean, sorry. I always get that mixed up. We're dotting the, the... we're putting the finishing touches on it. And of course that means, uh, dotting the t's and crossing the...we're almost done. Finishing it. And I think you're very good. Very attractive woman –

EDIE. Thank you.

VINCENT. You're perfect...for a lot of the...roles in the film. Oh, see, I wasn't supposed to say anything.

EDIE. It's a movie? Is it an independent?

VINCENT. Yes. Very independent. It's got a mind of its own this film. Not tied to any one, in any way, indicating any kind of...dependency. That's why, you saying it's an independent film, is exactly correct.

EDIE. But it's small-budget.

VINCENT. Not too small, but –

EDIE. Under a million?

VINCENT. Well, I'd say between a million and under a million – now, is it okay if I ask you a question?

EDIE. Sure.

VINCENT. Do you really handicap horses?

EDIE. How did you – Oh, it's down on there. No, not anymore. I haven't been to the track in years, but my father used to take me now and then. Why? Is it, does the movie have something to do with horses?

VINCENT. What movie? Oh, the movie, that movie, well, yes, in a sense it does, and then when I saw on your résumé that you were familiar with the track, with betting and all, I thought, I've got to give this girl a call.

EDIE. Wow, I'd love to hear more about it. Are you scouting for locations? 'Cause I used to know a couple of trainers

down at Aqueduct and they would get me up real
close –

VINCENT. Really?

EDIE. Sure. Of course I haven't been there in years, but I
could take you – I mean, I could, if you give me the
number of your location scout, I could tell him about it,
or...well, I guess I'm getting ahead of myself.

VINCENT. No, I appreciate your help –

EDIE. I could call him and –

VINCENT. Or maybe we could go. To the track sometime. To
do some scouting.

EDIE. Uh...sure. That'd be great. It's a lot of fun being there,
outside in the sun. Even if you don't bet, right?

VINCENT. I haven't been outside in a long time.

> *(The phone rings.)*

Oh, Good.

(Into the phone.) Centennial Casting. I mean, uh...no,
that's it, Centennial Casting. Hello, yes. Of course, I'll
check on that actor right now.

(To EDIE.*)* Excuse me, I have to take this.

EDIE. Oh, of course.

VINCENT. It was a pleasure meeting you.

> *(He tries to stretch the phone to walk her to
> the door.)*

EDIE. Yes, of course. Thank you for having me.

VINCENT. Can I call you? I mean, I'm sure I'll be calling you
again.

EDIE. I'd love to come in and read for you.

VINCENT. Oh, yes. That would be nice.

> *(He shakes her hand.)*

Very nice.

EDIE. Okay. Thank you again.

VINCENT. Edie. Thanks for coming in.

> *(She exits. He talks into the phone:)*

VINCENT. Mikey what the hell do you want? I sent you the damned thing already, can't you see I'm busy? Busy what? Busy casting!

(**DOO-DOO** *enters.*)

I'll call you later.

(*He hangs up.*)

DOO-DOO. How did it go?

VINCENT. She's beautiful.

DOO-DOO. You like her?

VINCENT. Doo, she bets the ponies.

DOO-DOO. For real?

VINCENT. No joke. She said she'd go to the track, give me some pointers.

DOO-DOO. No.

VINCENT. What am I gonna do?

DOO-DOO. What are you gonna do? You're gonna take her to the track and ride that filly home!

VINCENT. What am I gonna do when she finds out I'm not in showbiz?

DOO-DOO. Aw come on, why do you gotta be that way. This whole thing went really good. Vinnie, you think she likes you?

VINCENT. I think she likes Vincent DiDonato, casting guy.

DOO-DOO. Really?

VINCENT. Sure. She's an actress, right? The whole thing mighta been an act just so she could get a part.

DOO-DOO. You think?

VINCENT. I don't know, maybe.

DOO-DOO. In that case, we gotta get her a part in something.

VINCENT. Oh, yeah? And how we gonna do that?

DOO-DOO. Easy. We put on a show.

(*He looks at* **VINCENT**.)

(*Blackout.*)

Scene Six – The Diner

(The Moondance Diner. It is raining outside.
EDIE *and* **MICHELE** *are standing at opposite*
ends of the counter. **EDIE** *is staring at her cell*
phone.)

MICHELE. He said he'll call, he'll call.

EDIE. That was two weeks ago.

MICHELE. Maybe he's been busy.

EDIE. Maybe he was just feeding me a line. I don't know, I thought he liked me, but why would he? I cried to him on the phone, I got no credits to speak of, he must have thought I was a total loser.

MICHELE. He said he wanted you to come in and read.

EDIE. Yeah, yeah. Well, am I reading? No, I am sitting here, waiting. Waiting on his call, waiting on these frigging tables. Waiting, waiting, waiting...

MICHELE. Come on, forget about it.

EDIE. He seemed so...interested in me. He said I shimmered. Like a star.

MICHELE. Really.

EDIE. Yeah, he did.

(Pause.)

Centennial Casting.

MICHELE. What.

EDIE. Nothing, it's just...there's something funny about that place. It smells like my father's garage. And I don't even remember sending them a picture.

MICHELE. Big deal. You send out lots of pictures. What kind of stuff does he cast?

EDIE. He does movies. Right now he's casting an independent.

MICHELE. What's that, like soft porn?

EDIE. No, it's an independent feature film. It's low-budget.

MICHELE. So it's soft porn for no money.

Look, he called you in, you did your best and that's all you can do.

EDIE. *(Pause.)* I have to tell them by the end of the week.

MICHELE. Who them? Tell what?

EDIE. Tell them whether I want the job. In Ohio.

MICHELE. Don't start with this.

EDIE. I was feeling hopeful because of the stupid Centennial Casting audition, but now...
   Ah, screw it. *(Begins looking through her bag.)*

MICHELE. What are you doing?

EDIE. I'm calling right now and accepting the teaching job.

MICHELE. *(Grabs* **EDIE**'s *bag.)* No, you're not.

EDIE. Give me the bag.

MICHELE. You don't want to live in Ohio.

EDIE. Nobody does, but I'll do it anyway.

MICHELE. You'll go back to Kevin.

EDIE. I'll never go back to Kevin.

MICHELE. What if this casting guy calls with work? What do you say?

EDIE. I say, "I'm sorry, Vincent, I'm out of the business."

MICHELE. Wait...

EDIE. I'm moving to Ohio to teach drama at a lovely middle school, so I'm no longer available to do *Night of the Giving Head.*

MICHELE. Wait, what did you say?

EDIE. *Night of the Giving Head.*

MICHELE. No, what's his name?

EDIE. Whose name?

MICHELE. The guy.

EDIE. Vincent.

MICHELE. No, look at me.

EDIE. What.

MICHELE. Wow.

EDIE. What.

MICHELE. You like this guy, don't you?

EDIE. Who?

MICHELE. This guy, this casting guy.

EDIE. No.

MICHELE. You do.

EDIE. What are you talking about?

MICHELE. It's the way you say his name.

EDIE. You're crazy.

MICHELE. Edie, I have known every guy you liked since seventh grade. Say his name!

EDIE. Vincent.

MICHELE. No, see now you're trying to do less with it. Say it like you said it the first time.

EDIE. Vincent.

MICHELE. Try this. Say it like he just came into the room. Like I'm him, I walk in the room.

> *(She runs to the door and imitates him.)*

You say hello to me.

EDIE. Hello.

MICHELE. No, you gotta say, "Hello Vincent." Try it again.

> **(MICHELE** *runs to the door. Just then the door opens and in steps* **VINCENT**, *behind her.)*

EDIE. Hello Vincent.

MICHELE. That's it, that's the way you –

VINCENT. How's it going?

MICHELE. *(To* **VINCENT**.*)* – Hi.

EDIE. What are you doing here?

VINCENT. I was in the neighborhood, I thought I'd stop in for a coffee.

EDIE. Wow. Hello.

VINCENT. Hello. Hi, I'm Vincent.

> *(He holds his hand out to* **MICHELE**.*)*

EDIE. Oh, this is my friend, Michele.

VINCENT. How do you do?

MICHELE. I do just fine.

EDIE. Well, sit down, what can I get you?

VINCENT. No, I gotta run. Just coffee to go, cream, two sugars, please.

MICHELE. I'll get it.

EDIE. No, I got it.

MICHELE. I said I'd get it.

VINCENT. Hey, she's trying to weasel in on your tip.

EDIE. *(Laughing too hard.)* Oh, that's funny. Weasel in on my...yeah.

> (**MICHELE** *gets the cup.*)

VINCENT. So, how've you been?

EDIE. Good. Good. Keeping busy. You know how it is.

VINCENT. Yeah.

> *(Pause.)*

So, listen, I was going to call you but then I figured I'd stop by and tell you in person. We're doing this independent feature and I want you to come by and read for the director.

EDIE. Oh. Thank you.

VINCENT. Yeah. It's gonna be in the same place, our casting office.

EDIE. Great.

VINCENT. So, how's two o'clock on Friday?

EDIE. I'll be there. Are there sides?

VINCENT. No, either side is fine.

EDIE. *(Laughs.)* You're funny. I mean is there anything I have to prepare?

VINCENT. *(Covering for himself, he laughs as well.)* No, I just, no. Little joke there. Just come and we'll figure it out as we go.

EDIE. Great. Thanks.

MICHELE. *(Bringing coffee.)* Cream, two sugars.

VINCENT. Thanks.

MICHELE. Sure.

> (**MICHELE** *moves to the end of the counter, still in range.*)

VINCENT. So.

> (*Pause.*)

Moondance. Nice name for a diner.

EDIE. I think so.

VINCENT. Sounds kinda light, you know?

> (**EDIE** *smiles.*)

Okay, I gotta get going.

> (*He begins to leave.*)

EDIE. Excuse me, Vincent?

VINCENT. Yeah?

EDIE. What's the name of the film?

VINCENT. Oh. As of yet, it is untitled.

EDIE. I see. Well. Thanks. See you Friday.

VINCENT. See you Friday.

> (*He exits.*)

MICHELE. (*Moves next to* **EDIE**.) Untitled?

EDIE. Guess so.

MICHELE. Weird name for a porn flick.

> (**EDIE** *smacks* **MICHELE** *with her handbag.*)
>
> (*Blackout.*)

Scene Seven – The Office

> (**VINCENT** *sits at a long table, nervously tapping his fingers. He is sorting eight-by-tens, trying to make it look as if he knows what he's doing.*)

VINCENT. Actors, actors, there's too many actors. Where the hell's Edie?

> (*He rummages through the pictures on his desk.*)

Doo-Doo!

> (*He considers another picture from all angles and then finally tosses it under the desk.*)

Where the hell's Edie? Doo-Doo, where the hell's Edie's picture? Doo-Doo!

> (**DOO-DOO** *enters with a flourish. He is dressed like Otto Preminger, complete with riding crop, beret, and boots. He speaks with a heavy Italian accent.*)

DOO-DOO. Buon Giorno.

VINCENT. Doo-Doo, what the hell –

DOO-DOO. No no. I am Aldo.

VINCENT. Aldo?

DOO-DOO. No, say it with a flourish. Al-Do.

VINCENT. What's that mean?

DOO-DOO. It means I'm the director.

VINCENT. You look like a circus act.

DOO-DOO. This is how they dress.

VINCENT. Since when?

DOO-DOO. Ain't you ever seen *Sunset Boulevard*?

VINCENT. Doo, that was one hundred years ago.

DOO-DOO. I'm a throwback.

VINCENT. I oughta throw *you* back, in the frigging ocean. She's gonna take one look at you and run outta here.

DOO-DOO. You told me to dress the part.

VINCENT. Yeah, but –

DOO-DOO. Don't worry, I got it all figured out. I'm gonna be like the aloof producer/director person. A man of very few words, kind of like...a *mystery*!

VINCENT. So what's your last name, Aldo?

DOO-DOO. That's the whole thing.

VINCENT. It's one word.

DOO-DOO. One name is good. One name sounds... intellectual.

VINCENT. One name sounds stupid. You gotta have a last name.

DOO-DOO. Never mind. Just call me Aldo.

VINCENT. All right. What movie are you doing, Mr. Aldo?

DOO-DOO. Something foreign. A romance, but with a *touch of adventure.*

VINCENT. It's gotta be about horses. I told her it was about horses.

DOO-DOO. Don't worry, it's got horses. It's the story of two star-crossed lovers who fall in love at the racetrack. In Italy.

VINCENT. And it's called...

DOO-DOO. *(Thinking, and then.)* I got it. SEA-BISCOT!

VINCENT. What?

DOO-DOO. Sea-Biscot, get it?

VINCENT. That's stupid...

DOO-DOO. I like it and I'm the director. Here, read this. We gotta get ready for the audition. My nephew Joseph was gonna do this, but he couldn't make it. Hey Carmine!

VINCENT. Carmine?

> (**CARMINE** *walks in wearing a jockey costume. It is colorful and fits poorly.)*

DOO-DOO. Come on, get in here!

VINCENT. What's he doing here?

CARMINE. I'm the talent.

DOO-DOO. Okay, you remember your line?

CARMINE. I think so. I'm a little nervous.

DOO-DOO. How come?

CARMINE. I ain't never rode a horse before.

DOO-DOO. Okay. Let's do a little what they call the sense memories.

> (**DOO-DOO** *stands beside* **CARMINE**, *who stares ahead, visualizing the different locales, expressing joy, fear, and his childhood.*)

Imagine you're five years old and your father takes you to the amusement park. There are many rides at the amusement park, the Ferris wheel, the Tilt-A-Whirl, the haunted house, and there, in the distance, the merry-go-round. He places you on the biggest horse, a valiant charger! He straps you in...

VINCENT. WHAT THE HELL ARE YOU DOING?

DOO-DOO. I'm getting him ready.

CARMINE. I was just getting into it.

> (*There's a knock at the door.*)

DOO-DOO. Shit, that's her.

VINCENT. Wait, I can't do this.

DOO-DOO. You gotta do it.

VINCENT. I can't.

DOO-DOO. Answer the door.

VINCENT. I'm gonna tell her the truth.

DOO-DOO. Don't worry, it's all gonna work.

VINCENT. But what if it don't?

DOO-DOO. Trust me! Get the door.

VINCENT. You get it.

DOO-DOO. I can't get it. I'm the director.

CARMINE. What do I do?

DOO-DOO. *(With a flourish.)* Prepare!

> (**CARMINE** *fumbles and then strikes a "jockey at the ready" pose.*)

VINCENT. Jesus.

> (**VINCENT** *opens the door.*)

EDIE. Hi.

VINCENT. Hello again.

EDIE. I hope you don't mind I'm early.

VINCENT. Not at all, come in. Have a seat.

(*He pulls up a chair for her.*)

Oh, allow me to introduce my associate.

(**DOO-DOO**, *who has had his back to them, facing the wall, now turns around with a flourish.*)

DOO-DOO. I am Aldo.

EDIE. Hi Aldo.

(**DOO-DOO** *kisses her hand.*)

My goodness.

VINCENT. Yeah, goodness. Why don't we get started?

EDIE. That's fine. Um, I was told there weren't any sides.

DOO-DOO. Oh no, I do not believe in what you call the sides.

EDIE. I see.

DOO-DOO. Carmine!

CARMINE. Hmm?

DOO-DOO. This is Carmine.

EDIE. Hello. Oh, I saw your work the other day. Nice to see you again.

(**CARMINE** *nods intently.*)

DOO-DOO. We are going to do, what we call in my country, an Im-PRO-visa-TION.

EDIE. Oh, Improv sure.

VINCENT. You know all about that?

EDIE. Yeah, I've done lots of that.

DOO-DOO. Basta!

(**DOO-DOO** *puts his arm around* **CARMINE**.)

Carmine is a jockey and he has ridden many horses to victory. But his last race, he had a bad fall. And now, just before the big race, he is very, how you say, afraid to get back on the horse, Sea-BISCOT! But you, you are his love and you must convince him that to win your love, he must ride again!

EDIE. And the horse is named Sea...

DOO-DOO. BISCOT!

EDIE. This is a joke, right?

VINCENT. Forget the name. Let's just get on with the...

EDIE. Sure, I'll give it a go.

DOO-DOO. Very good.

Action!

(He claps his hands together.)

CARMINE. *(Very stiff, looks to* **DOO-DOO** *for assurance.)* I can't do it. I can't get back on that horse!

EDIE. Come on Carmine, you gotta!

CARMINE. *(Pause.)* I can't do it. I can't get back on that horse!

DOO-DOO. Cut! Carmine, you must show...how you say, more fright, more terror, capisce?

CARMINE. Okay.

DOO-DOO. *(To* **EDIE**.*)* You...you are very good!

EDIE. Thanks.

DOO-DOO. But I need more...passion! Capisce?

EDIE. I think so.

DOO-DOO. Passion. Mmm.

(He claps his hands again.)

Action!

CARMINE. I can't do it. I can't get back on that horse!

EDIE. Carmine, I believe in you, I know you can do it this time!

DOO-DOO. No, no, no, there needs to be passion. You see?

VINCENT. Hold on a second!

DOO-DOO. Aspetta! *[Meaning "wait."]* I am creating! I am the art-teest, si?

VINCENT. Well –

DOO-DOO. Sush!

> *(To* **EDIE**.*)* He must ride on Sea-BISCOT! And you are the only one who can give him the strength to carry on! Si?

EDIE. I see.

DOO-DOO. Good. Very good.

> *(Claps his hands.)*

Action!

CARMINE. I can't do it. I can't get on –

EDIE. *(Suddenly finding her voice.)* All right, listen pal. I love you and I love that horse. And I don't care if I have to jump up on him and ride him myself, but he's running today and he's gonna win. Now you get up in that saddle or I'm gonna kick your ass in front of all your five-foot friends! Now get on Seabiscot and you ride, ride, ride!

DOO-DOO. Bravo. Bravisimo! Very good.

> *(To* **VINCENT**.*)* Was very good, no?

VINCENT. Perfect.

CARMINE. That was excellent.

VINCENT. Fine. Well I think we've seen enough, right Aldo?

> *(***DOO-DOO** *closes his eyes, deep in thought.)*

I think that's a yes.

EDIE. Well, great.

VINCENT. Thanks for coming in.

EDIE. Sure.

VINCENT. It was great, really.

> *(***VINCENT** *takes* **EDIE** *off to one side.)*

You did good. I mean, I really liked what you did last time and uh...that's why I wanted to call you in to meet Mr., uh...Mr. Aldo.

EDIE. Is he all right?

VINCENT. He's just thinking of the old country. Listen, it was great seeing you again.

DOO-DOO. Aspetta. If you please, when do you get to do the...how you say, research?

VINCENT. What research?

DOO-DOO. At the...aqua duck? So we can see the horses, yes?

VINCENT. Oh. Yes. Actually, uh...Edie...Miss Keaton, you knew something about that, didn't you?

EDIE. The track? Sure.

VINCENT. I had somebody else was supposed to take me out there to do some, how you call it, scouting, but it fell through. So maybe, you think you have time to maybe, show me around?

EDIE. Of course.

VINCENT. Just to do research, you understand?

EDIE. That'd be great.

VINCENT. So how about tomorrow? They run 'em on Saturday.

EDIE. Okay.

VINCENT. What do you say I pick you up at the Moondance, say noontime?

EDIE. I'd love it. See you then.

VINCENT. Okay.

EDIE. Thanks again.

(*To* **DOO-DOO.**) Ciao!

(*She exits.*)

VINCENT. What the hell were you doing?

DOO-DOO. You know, she wasn't bad! Would you offer her the part?

VINCENT. In what?

DOO-DOO. In my movie.

VINCENT. Doo-Doo, you ain't got a movie!

CARMINE. How was I?

VINCENT. What?

CARMINE. Was my character specific enough?

VINCENT. Get the hell out of here!

(**CARMINE** *exits with a sniffle.*)

DOO-DOO. At first I thought she was too timid, but then when she let him have it, I'll tell you Vinnie, this is quite a girl. You know what it is? She ain't built for speed, she's built to last.

VINCENT. That's for sure.

DOO-DOO. But is that right for the part?

VINCENT. Cut the shit. I'm in big trouble here.

DOO-DOO. What are you talking?

VINCENT. Tomorrow, we got a date at the track –

DOO-DOO. That's great!

VINCENT. And what do I do when she starts asking about the movie?

DOO-DOO. You don't say nothing. You just wait a coupla weeks and then you call her up one day and say, "Oh, I'm sorry, somebody else got the part," and then you just drop it.

VINCENT. She's gonna see right through that.

DOO-DOO. No she won't. Later on, if things work out and you guys hit it off, then you just conveniently get out of the business and that'll be the part of your past you gotta lie about.

VINCENT. But that's just it, I don't wanna lie to her.

DOO-DOO. Hey, you already lied this much.

VINCENT. Doo-Doo –

DOO-DOO. Vinnie you want this? You gotta work for it. Sometimes working for it means...you gotta stretch the truth a little. Do you want this Vinnie?

VINCENT. Yeah. More than anything.

DOO-DOO. All right then. You go to the track tomorrow, have a good time and who knows? Maybe you'll hit her daily doubles.

VINCENT. And when can I tell her the truth?

DOO-DOO. After she falls in love with you.

(*Blackout.*)

Scene Eight – The Track

(VINCENT and EDIE stand near the rail at Aqueduct Racetrack. In the darkness, we hear the ANNOUNCER.)

ANNOUNCER. *(Offstage.)* Two minutes to post!

EDIE. See you need to be down this close to take a good look at the horses. I mean, if the character is a jockey and he's on the mend, he would hang around the paddock and the stables. But from here you get a good sense of how the horse is riding.

VINCENT. Uh-huh.

EDIE. You get a good look at how heavily muscled the horse is, get a sense of how he walks, tail off his rump, that kind of thing.

VINCENT. Right. Thank you. That'll be a big help, I think. Very useful information. So, tell me, who do you like?

(He shows her the program.)

EDIE. I don't know. You want to bet?

VINCENT. Hey, why not, we're here.

EDIE. Okay. Be fun.

VINCENT. I like Emerson's Boozer.

EDIE. Really?

VINCENT. Yeah, why?

EDIE. Nothing. I like…Big City Dance.

VINCENT. Big City Dance. 5-1. Why him?

EDIE. He ran well here last time, track is kind of slow, he likes the mud. Makes sense to me. Why do you like… what was the name again?

VINCENT. Emerson's Boozer. Uh…well…my mother liked the Jets.

EDIE. Uh-huh.

VINCENT. He was a running back –

EDIE. You can't bet the horse's name.

VINCENT. That's what I always do.

EDIE. Vincent, you've got a lot to learn. But that's why they run 'em, right?

VINCENT. Sure. This is fun. I'm glad we came out here.

EDIE. Me too.

VINCENT. Haven't been to the track since I was a kid. My mother used to take me all the time.

EDIE. That's funny. My dad used to take me, too.

VINCENT. Okay, so, I'm gonna place these –

EDIE. You know, I'm really excited about the movie.

VINCENT. Yeah, me too.

EDIE. To tell you the truth, I was getting ready to quit the business.

VINCENT. Oh?

EDIE. Yeah. I had this other job offer, running a drama club at a middle school in Ohio –

VINCENT. Really.

EDIE. And I was this close to taking it. But last night, after auditioning for Aldo, I called them and told them, "No." I'm gonna stick with this. Acting. I just feel like something's gonna happen. Something good.

VINCENT. I got that feeling too.

(There is a pause. They exchange a look, starting to fall for each other, and then:)

Edie. I gotta tell you something.

EDIE. I gotta tell you something, too.

VINCENT. You go first.

EDIE. Well, this is a little embarrassing, and I don't even know why I'm telling you this but this audition thing, it's always been really hard for me...

VINCENT. But you were terrific yesterday.

EDIE. That's the thing. I was. At least I think I was. At least I think I was as good as I could be. I gave a good audition, didn't I?

VINCENT. I can't imagine anyone better.

EDIE. It felt good. And it gave me the feeling that maybe, just maybe the curse has been lifted.

VINCENT. Curse? What curse?

EDIE. I'm not gonna get all voodoo on you, but you see, three years ago, just before I quit the business, I had an audition at the Folger. Do you ever work with the Folger?

VINCENT. Not that I recall.

EDIE. And I was auditioning for Felix LaSalle.

VINCENT. Ah, Felix.

EDIE. Yeah, so I was auditioning for Kate from *Shrew* and right when I got to the part where "a woman moved is like a fountain troubled" Felix LaSalle starts yelling at me, screaming at me, really, telling me what a terrible job I'm doing, how dare I have the audacity to speak the words of the Bard in his presence...

VINCENT. What a schmuck.

EDIE. ...And then he got so upset he started coughing and he started sputtering and his face got kind of red and purple and maroon, really, and he was reaching, reaching towards me and then, well...

VINCENT. Yeah?

EDIE. He died.

VINCENT. Dead?

EDIE. He did. Right there in front of me. On top of me, actually. He sort of fell on me. And died.

VINCENT. Oh, jeez.

EDIE. And I tried to roll him over to give him mouth-to-mouth or whatever, but he was a big guy, 250, 260, maybe and I was stuck, somehow, under him and I was yelling call 911, call 911! I mean later they told me his heart was the size of a volleyball and he'd just had three Big Macs for breakfast. But still, it was awful. And from that moment on, whenever I auditioned, I felt I was cursed. All I kept hearing in my head were his last words, "Miss Keaton, your acting is killing me." So ever since then, I'd go to an audition and I'd...freeze. Just freeze...until I met you. Vincent.

VINCENT. What are ya talking?

EDIE. Remember when I was doing Lady M for you and you started coughing?

VINCENT. Holy crap.

EDIE. I was like no, not again! It can't be happening again!

VINCENT. Oh, I'm sorry, I didn't –

EDIE. No, no, it wasn't you, Vincent. It was me. It was me, absolutely sure that I was going to screw it up again. Because I suck. I suck so bad that people actually die from my suckiness.

VINCENT. Edie...

EDIE. But then you called me back. And I auditioned for Aldo. And it went...well. Didn't it?

VINCENT. It did.

EDIE. So I think the curse is over. I think you broke the curse for me. And I just want to thank you.

  (She smiles. A beautiful smile.)

VINCENT. I think you're gonna go far, Edie. I really do. You have a lot of talent. And I look forward to seeing you more. I mean, more of you. I mean, see you do more. Acting.

EDIE. Thanks, Vincent. Now, you wanted to tell me something?

VINCENT. Huh?

EDIE. You had something to tell me, before I went on and on about my tale of woe.

VINCENT. Oh. Oh. Yeah. It's just that...listen, Edie.

  *(He looks at **EDIE**...is he about to tell her?)*

The truth is...I been having kind of a bad luck streak, too.

EDIE. Really?

VINCENT. Yeah. Yeah. See, I ain't picked a winner in years.

EDIE. Well. Well, maybe that's about to change.

VINCENT. Maybe.

>   *(Pause.)*

All right, I'd better get to the window. Wait...who do you like again?

EDIE. *(Leans over. Looks at the form.)* Who do I like? I don't know. I don't see his name here.

VINCENT. Who are you looking for?

EDIE. Somebody strong. Somebody with a lotta heart. Somebody who won't quit on me.

VINCENT. Could be a winner.

>   **(EDIE** *and* **VINCENT** *look at each other. Are they going to kiss? After a moment, we hear the bell ring, but neither one turns to the track.)*

ANNOUNCER. *(Offstage.)* And they're off!

>   *(Blackout.)*

ACT TWO

Scene One – The Diner

*(**EDIE** is wiping the counter. **MICHELE** is looking at some postcards. It is late in the evening.)*

MICHELE. It's totally wrong.

EDIE. I'm not seeing it.

MICHELE. Look closely.

EDIE. What am I looking for?

MICHELE. Just look!

EDIE. "Sequoia Gallery, contemporary metal sculptures."

MICHELE. Yeah?

EDIE. Michele Bates. They spelled your name right.

MICHELE. Look at the dragonflies.

EDIE. The dragonflies.

MICHELE. They're supposed to be adjacent. Like they're flying off into the distance. Does it look like they're flying to you?

(Pause.)

EDIE. It looks like they're screwing.

MICHELE. Yes! Who's gonna come to a show where there's dragonflies screwing?

EDIE. Do dragonflies screw or do they lay eggs?

MICHELE. They screw, then they lay eggs – who cares?! It's wrong for the show. And it's supposed to match the insignia of the dopey software company.

EDIE. Sorry, Mish.

MICHELE. How the hell am I gonna get these back to the copy place before they close? I'll never make it.

EDIE. Just go now, I'll close up.

MICHELE. Really?

EDIE. Sure, go ahead.

MICHELE. Thanks, hun. I owe ya.

EDIE. I'm waiting for Vincent, anyway.

MICHELE. You're what?

EDIE. Waiting for Vincent. We're going out for dessert.

MICHELE. You went out last night.

EDIE. Yeah.

MICHELE. And the night before.

EDIE. So?

MICHELE. So what are you doing?

EDIE. I think it's called dating.

MICHELE. You can't be doing that. He's a caster guy.

EDIE. He's sweet.

MICHELE. Sweet, huh? I don't trust him.

EDIE. You don't trust anybody.

MICHELE. Yeah, well maybe you could use a little more of that...wariness.

EDIE. I didn't ask you, did I?

MICHELE. No, you didn't. But –

EDIE. Good. End of discussion.

MICHELE. Is he dating you? Or getting you a job? Not a good idea, Edie. Not a good idea to mix business with pleasure.

EDIE. You're gonna be late.

MICHELE. What I'm trying to say is –

EDIE. Yeah?

          *(**VINCENT** enters.)*

MICHELE. Don't shit where you eat!

VINCENT. Good advice.

MICHELE. Oh, hello.

VINCENT. How you doin'?

EDIE. Hello Vincent. Mish was just leaving.

VINCENT. We'll miss you.

EDIE. *(To* **MICHELE.***)* You got twenty minutes.

(To **VINCENT.***)* It's her cards. For her show. They messed up big time.

VINCENT. Huh?

MICHELE. Here. Take a look. *(Takes out a card.)*

VINCENT. Okay.

MICHELE. What does that look like to you?

(Pause.)

VINCENT. It looks like two dragonflies screwing.

EDIE. Bye Mish.

VINCENT. Did I say something wrong?

MICHELE. Good bye. *(Gathering the postcards.)* Have fun. HEY!

VINCENT. What?

MICHELE. *(Slight pause.)* Behave!

(She exits.)

VINCENT. Nice girl.

EDIE. She is.

VINCENT. Hey, I got something for you.

(He takes out a small box, hands it to her.)

EDIE. Oh...

VINCENT. It's no big deal or nothing, just a little...I don't know.

(Pulls bracelet out and helps her put it on.)

Some guy on the street was selling them and it made me think of you. I like that stuff on the street. Looks all kinda unique, you know?

EDIE. Oh, it's got horses.

VINCENT. Yeah, sort of looks like two fillies being chased by two thoroughbreds.

EDIE. I love it. Thank you, Vincent.

VINCENT. You're welcome.

> *(Pause.)*

Nice in here. All quiet and all.

EDIE. It is. Hey, we don't have to go out. We got the whole place to ourselves and I got cheesecake in the walk-in. You like cheesecake?

VINCENT. Do I look like I like cheesecake?

EDIE. Be right back.

VINCENT. I was thinking of going on the Atkins. Did you know you could eat cheesecake on the Atkins? Gonna try to lose a pound or two. I don't know. Just thinking about it.

EDIE. *(Returning.)* I think you look great.

VINCENT. Thanks. So that was fun, last night. I enjoyed that play. Very much.

EDIE. Me too. It was interesting. I never thought of Othello as a white woman. But somehow it worked.

VINCENT. It did. It did.

EDIE. Yeah, you know I've always dreamed of playing Desdemona.

VINCENT. Really...

EDIE. Oh, yeah. Actually, it was the first scene I ever worked on. I signed up for this class and my teacher gave me Desdemona and I was...I don't know...hooked, I guess. *(Holds up the bracelet.)* Thanks again, Vincent. Did I say thank you?

VINCENT. You did. Edie, I gotta tell you. I've enjoyed these past three weeks so much.

EDIE. Me too.

VINCENT. Really?

EDIE. Oh, yeah. I mean, you're the first guy I've spent time with, really, since my divorce. And you're terrific, Vincent. Really. I don't know why someone hasn't scooped you up long ago.

VINCENT. I was almost scooped up. Once.

EDIE. Just once?

VINCENT. Just once. Long time ago.

EDIE. Well, it's her loss, Vincent. Truly.

VINCENT. We dated a long time. Eleven, twelve years. Then she left me. For the cable guy.

EDIE. Yeesh, that musta hurt.

VINCENT. It did. I couldn't watch HBO for months. It was my fault, I just couldn't seem to make her happy. And then after a while, you just get used to living alone. And you forget that there's any other way to live.

EDIE. I know what you mean. I do.

(*Pause.*)

It's nice to meet a guy like you after the disaster that I married.

VINCENT. Didn't work out, huh?

EDIE. First of all I shoulda known when he told me I was a rotten actress, this was not the guy for me. Mmm, good cheesecake, huh? After he saw me in a showcase of "A Thousand Clowns" he asked me to marry him on the condition that I quit acting.

VINCENT. He didn't say that.

EDIE. He did. Took me in his arms, kissed me and said, "Edie, you couldn't act dead if you was."

VINCENT. Ah, what does he know?

EDIE. But it wasn't that as much as the lies that he told me. His lies. If there's one thing I cannot tolerate it's a liar.

VINCENT. Yeah.

EDIE. He said he was a big-time real estate agent, had a good job in Ohio, would I please move there with him. So me, I packed up, got rid of my apartment, which he had been living in, by the way, quit the business and married him. We get there and is he a big-time real estate agent? No, he is not. He's the janitor of a building. Not that there's anything wrong with that. But he got me out there under false pretenses. How could I ever trust him again?

VINCENT. You couldn't.

EDIE. And that was just one of the lies. Saying he wasn't drinking, when he was. Saying there weren't other women, when there were. So I hightailed it out of Ohio, finally, and landed on Mish's couch. She got me the job at the diner and that's where I've been the past eighteen months. But, who knows, maybe I'll get cast in this movie and it'll be a big hit? Have you heard anything from Aldo?

VINCENT. Aldo? Oh no, not yet.

EDIE. I don't mean to be pushy, but –

VINCENT. Oh not at all. See Aldo is very particular, and... see, he wanted to talk to you himself. Because he was very impressed with your audition.

EDIE. Really?

VINCENT. Yes. But sadly...he's been called away.

EDIE. To where?

VINCENT. To his villa. In faraway Italy.

EDIE. Italy?

VINCENT. Yes. He had to leave, very suddenly. Some sort of Italian emergency over there...in a remote site, near his villa...in faraway Italy.

EDIE. I hope it's nothing too serious.

VINCENT. It could be serious. But right now, we're just not sure.

EDIE. Oh.

VINCENT. I would rather that you heard it from him directly. It'll probably be next week sometime. Or maybe the week after. Who knows? You know how these Italian emergencies can be.

EDIE. Oh, I understand. It's just that I've actually got a callback to do dinner theatre in Florida this summer.

VINCENT. Oh.

EDIE. I can't believe it, but I'm out there, auditioning. Thanks to you.

VINCENT. What other auditions do you have?

EDIE. Well, Utah Shakespeare Festival is doing an open call for *Othello*. That's why I wanted to see it last night. I've always dreamed of playing Desdemona.

VINCENT. Utah? Why would you want to go out there?

EDIE. It's a great theater, great reputation. Do you do much casting for regionals?

VINCENT. Nah, not much. So you would do that, you would go to Utah and Florida?

EDIE. Sure, why do you ask?

VINCENT. Nothing, I just thought of you as a...New York actress.

EDIE. Hey, you go where the work is, right?

VINCENT. Yeah.

(*Pause.*)

Edie, listen, maybe I'm not supposed to say anything...

EDIE. What.

VINCENT. I was gonna wait till I heard definitely from Aldo, but I think, uh...

EDIE. What??

VINCENT. I think he's gonna use you.

EDIE. You're kidding!

VINCENT. Yeah. Maybe. He wants to read you one more time.

EDIE. I haven't even read from the script yet.

VINCENT. Well, that's the thing. That's what's holding him back, because the script is...it's coming from overseas and it's not done yet, not really.

EDIE. They're still making changes.

VINCENT. That's right. It has to be translated from the Italian and I'm supposed to set up something, another, how you call it, a read-through for you to read from the script...for him. But I can't do that, until he gets over here.

EDIE. I'm so happy.

VINCENT. It'll probably be next week sometime. Or maybe the week after.

EDIE. Okay.

VINCENT. Good. Good.

>   *(Pause.)*

Listen, Edie. It's tough, this casting business.

EDIE. It is.

VINCENT. Getting tougher all the time out there. In fact, I was toying with the idea of leaving. You know? Giving up the business.

EDIE. How come?

VINCENT. Ahh, it's a rat race. I never really understood how a lot of things worked and I kinda backed into this and…I don't know. Would you care?

EDIE. What do you mean?

VINCENT. Would it matter to you if I did something else?

EDIE. Of course not.

VINCENT. Good.

EDIE. How could you say that?

VINCENT. I didn't mean –

EDIE. You think I'm going out with you because you're in casting?

VINCENT. No, but…you know how it is.

EDIE. No, I don't.

VINCENT. A lot of times, people do that. They go to all kinds of, how you call it, extremes to get what they want. I'm not saying that you would do that, but I know a lot of people who would. You know. There's a lot of uh…false people. In the world.

>   *(Pause.)*

EDIE. Hey.

>   *(She takes his face and kisses him.)*

I'm not one of 'em.

VINCENT. I know.

>   *(Blackout.)*

Scene Two – The Office

(The office of Centennial Casting. The movie posters and pictures are still up, but some small metal shop items have found their way in. **CARMINE** *is looking through folders while* **DOO-DOO** *sits at the desk reading* Variety. **VINCENT** *paces about.)*

VINCENT. Maybe if I just left town for a while.

CARMINE. Tool moldings, brake moldings –

VINCENT. Like I had to go on business or something and then I come back...

CARMINE. More brake moldings.

VINCENT. ...And while I was away, I had some kind of a what do you call it –

CARMINE. A brake molding.

VINCENT. A what?

CARMINE. Brake molding. Remember we got that big order that time from Napa, whatever it is?

VINCENT. What are you talking about?

CARMINE. Housings. You know boss, if we got computerized, we wouldn't have to do this.

VINCENT. What? Get outta here, I'm trying to think!

CARMINE. I gotta find the –

VINCENT. Get out!

(Looking close to tears, **CARMINE** *exits.)*

DOO-DOO. Now was that necessary?

VINCENT. I'm trying to think Doo.

DOO-DOO. And he's trying to work.

VINCENT. What do you call it when –

DOO-DOO. You remember work, don'tcha?

VINCENT. Never mind that. What do you call it when you go away –

DOO-DOO. Vacation.

VINCENT. No, when you go away, and you come back and like you have a whole different take on things.

DOO-DOO. A catharsis.

VINCENT. You had one of those?

DOO-DOO. Sure. Remember when I went to Vegas? Made me realize it's a good thing I work for a living.

VINCENT. I think it's gotta be something more serious.

DOO-DOO. What about a near-death experience?

VINCENT. That's it. I went away, on a working vacation, I had to leave suddenly. And there was this car accident and I almost lost my life and I had a near-death experience and I decided to leave the casting business.

DOO-DOO. You shouldn't talk like that.

VINCENT. Why not?

DOO-DOO. It could happen.

VINCENT. Ah, come on.

DOO-DOO. Besides, who would run the shop if you left the business?

VINCENT. Not this business, you moron. The casting business. Like actors, right?

DOO-DOO. Oh. Why would you do that? I thought you liked it.

VINCENT. Doo-Doo, would you cut the shit?

DOO-DOO. We were just about to make our first feature and everything.

VINCENT. I'm in big trouble here. I'm falling in love with this girl and she thinks I'm something I'm not.

DOO-DOO. You're kidding.

VINCENT. No.

DOO-DOO. You're in love?

VINCENT. Yeah. I think. Yeah.

DOO-DOO. Oh boy.

VINCENT. I know.

DOO-DOO. All right. There's only one thing to do. You gotta tell her the truth.

VINCENT. I've been trying to do that for three weeks now, but I can't. She'll hate me for the rest of her life.

DOO-DOO. Vinnie, you're running out of room, you know?

VINCENT. I like my vacation idea.

DOO-DOO. When you going to do this?

VINCENT. I gotta do it soon. She thinks she's meeting Aldo next week to read for the movie.

DOO-DOO. Well, Aldo has definitely left the building.

(He starts out the door.)

VINCENT. Come on Doo, you gotta help me. This was your idea.

DOO-DOO. Help you what? I got you set up with the girl, I never figured it would get this outta hand. Look, get lost for a while, go to Atlantic City or something. Give you some time to figure out a story. And then when you come back, who knows, maybe you can tell her you quit and she'll buy it.

VINCENT. You think?

DOO-DOO. No. But hey, it'll buy you some time, right? I gotta get this order out the door.

(He exits.)

VINCENT. Atlantic City. All right, not bad.

(He begins digging for the yellow pages.)

Looking for the big casino bus. Yeah, this'll work. Spend a week shooting craps...and I'll figure the whole thing...here we go.

(He begins dialing numbers.)

Yes, hello. I'd like to know when you have tour buses –

*(As he begins his call, **EDIE** walks in. She is carrying a big bouquet of flowers with a picnic basket. She is decked out, as if on a date.)*

– Uh...going to...

EDIE. Hey. *(Whispers.)* Don't let me interrupt.

VINCENT. Uh...no. NO, as a matter of fact – I mean yes, we can definitely do lunch. This week I'm all jammed up, but I bet we can do next Friday, how is that? Wonderful. Kiss kiss. Yeah. Good bye. *(Hangs up.)*

EDIE. Hi.

VINCENT. What are you doing here?

EDIE. Is this a bad time?

VINCENT. No, not at all –

EDIE. Whoa, this place looks different.

VINCENT. What? Oh, yeah, right. We're in the process of finally moving.

EDIE. Really? You didn't say –

VINCENT. Well, we finally found a place. A place in midtown. We had been waiting to hear if the lease would come through and it just came through yesterday so we're starting to take things apart and that's why things are such a mess. Whatcha got there?

EDIE. Nothing. Just some flowers to brighten things up.

VINCENT. Aw, that's sweet of you.

EDIE. *(Noticing some casting items, tools, and parts on the desk.)* Let's just move these – what the hell is this?

VINCENT. Huh? Oh, those are props. We were having a reading this morning of a film that uh...some actors came in, it's about a guy who works in a brake shop. Funny story, I don't really know if uh – let me get these out of the way. This is a surprise.

EDIE. Yeah, I brought you lunch.

VINCENT. What are you talking?

EDIE. I thought we'd go by the river and have a picnic.

VINCENT. Hey, that's great.

EDIE. I made you some eggplant like you like. I got some wine.

VINCENT. In the middle of the day?

EDIE. Why not? Come on, let's get out of here.

VINCENT. Okay, let me get my coat.

EDIE. So wait, this is a movie about a brake shop?

VINCENT. Yeah. It's a very wacky project. There's plumbers that come by and they're serial killers, it's crazy. You know what, let me tell you on the way.

(As they head for the door, **CARMINE** *busts in from the shop.)*

CARMINE. Vincent, I'd like a word with you.

VINCENT. Not now Carmine.

CARMINE. No, I've been very respectful of you in your time of need. But in all the time I worked for your mother, not once did she ever raise her voice to me, for I loved her like a mother.

VINCENT. Yeah, I know. Now –

CARMINE. Like the poet says, "Respect must be mutual."

VINCENT. That's very good Carmine. You keep working on that delivery, but remember, character comes from the *cojones*, right?

CARMINE. What?

(He notices **EDIE.***)*

Oh, right. Hello Miss Keaton, how are you today?

EDIE. Hi Carmine. What are you working on?

CARMINE. Oh. It's a –

VINCENT. A monologue.

CARMINE. A monomalagog…mono…what they call it when you talk alone.

EDIE. What's it from?

CARMINE. I'm not certain. That's why I'm having such difficulty with it.

(Just then, **DOO-DOO** *enters holding a brake fitting. He wears a welding mask, so he doesn't notice* **EDIE.***)*

DOO-DOO. Vinnie, Jesus Christ. This one ain't it either. We must have pressed this thing a dozen times and we can't get the specs right and now I look and I'm using the wrong fucking molding. Even though it's marked right here, what does that say. Read that. Right on the bottom there. Am I fucking blind or what? What the fuck does that say?

(Finally noticing **EDIE**.*)*

Oh. Hi.

EDIE. Aldo?

DOO-DOO. Buon Giorno!

EDIE. Wait a minute.

CARMINE. I gotta go.

(He exits hurriedly.)

DOO-DOO. Arrivederci!

VINCENT. Doo-Doo.

EDIE. Who?

VINCENT. Doo-Doo, get back here!

EDIE. What did you just call him?

VINCENT. Doo-Doo. That's his nickname. His real name is Alfonse. In fact he was the one who picked out your picture and résumé. See?

(He moves to the other side of the desk.)

See, we got a bunch of them. 'Cause sometimes, a lot of people think this is a casting office. But really, I mean, we do, do casting. Doo-Doo. Funny, I said it, Doo-Doo. Anyway, sometimes people thought we were in the theatre business, doing plays and things. When really all we do is make metal parts and things. Wrenches, screwdrivers, tools, you know? But we had a whole stack of these pictures, see? And yours came to my attention, especially since you liked the horses, you know? I thought, hey, this girl likes the horses, I'd like to meet her. So we kind of uh...set this whole thing up.

(Pause.)

I'm sorry, I didn't mean to hurt you.

EDIE. You lied to me?

VINCENT. I didn't know what else to do. I'm sorry. Edie.

EDIE. Stupid. I'm so stupid. You'd think I woulda learned, but no. I wanted to believe it so bad. I knew it. I knew it couldn't be true. You be honest with people, you tell the truth, and they just end up screwing you.

> *(She takes the flowers and slams them against the wall, breaking the vase.)*

VINCENT. That's not it.

EDIE. Yeah, what is it? Did you have a good laugh? Did you have your fun?

VINCENT. That's not why I did it.

EDIE. I turned down a real job for this. I turned down Dental!

> *(**EDIE** drops the picnic basket. She slaps **VINCENT**. She exits.)*
>
> *(After a moment, **DOO-DOO** walks downstage and picks up the basket. He begins to clean up the mess. **VINCENT** does not move. **DOO-DOO** notices an eggplant sandwich. He opens the sandwich and motions to **VINCENT**, "Do you want a bite?" **VINCENT** doesn't respond. **DOO-DOO** takes a bite out of the sandwich and continues to clean up.)*
>
> *(Blackout.)*

Scene Three – The Office

*(Two days later. **VINCENT** sits at the desk. He is unshaven and it looks as if he hasn't slept. He has a half-eaten box of cannolis in front of him and a cup of coffee in a cardboard cup. There are assorted empty pastry boxes strewn about. **DOO-DOO** sits at the corner of the desk. He has a small portion mapped out and is trying to do some work.)*

DOO-DOO. Okay. Six on each, one hundred to a case is, what, six hundred pieces to a case. Right?

> *(Pause.)*

Right. Times three hundred cases is...is, I need the calculator.

VINCENT. What?

DOO-DOO. I need the calculator. I'm trying to finish out this order.

VINCENT. 180,000.

DOO-DOO. You sure?

VINCENT. Yeah, 180k.

DOO-DOO. How do you figure?

VINCENT. Six times three is eighteen. Two zeros on each, 180,000. Anybody could figure it out.

DOO-DOO. Uh-huh. Well let me ask you this. How many cannolis come in a box.

VINCENT. A dozen.

DOO-DOO. Times four boxes is what, forty-eight cannolis.

VINCENT. You had a couple.

DOO-DOO. I had one.

VINCENT. So what's your point?

DOO-DOO. So what's your point? What the hell are you doing?

VINCENT. Eating.

DOO-DOO. You're digging your grave with that frigging ricotta. *[Pronounced RI-GOT.]*

VINCENT. What do you care?

DOO-DOO. By the time Saint Joseph's day comes around, you're gonna look like a giant zeppole. All right fine. You wanna eat that shit till you explode, be my guest. I got a shop to run. You remember the shop. We make stuff in it? Tools, fittings, crappy screwdriver parts.

VINCENT. Yeah, yeah, fine.

DOO-DOO. Vinnie, she's just a girl. You can't be going over the deep end here.

VINCENT. She was more than that. She was special. How many special girls you think you meet in your life?

DOO-DOO. Plenty.

VINCENT. Yeah? Well I ain't.

DOO-DOO. All right fine. So this is the girl for you?

VINCENT. What I'm saying.

DOO-DOO. You'd do anything for her?

VINCENT. Of course.

DOO-DOO. Beg, borrow, steal, lie?

VINCENT. I've done enough lying.

DOO-DOO. All right, wrong category. When my third wife left me the second time, you know what my father said to me? Four simple words. Get. Her. Back.

VINCENT. That's three words.

DOO-DOO. I think he was counting the exclamation point.

VINCENT. All right fine, get her back. How do I do that?

DOO-DOO. You get on your knees and you walk all the way from here to that stupid Moonshine Diner she works at and you beg her forgiveness.

VINCENT. That ain't gonna work.

DOO-DOO. How do you know?

VINCENT. She won't see me. She don't return my calls. She sees me on my knees walking up to her, she'll go out the back door.

DOO-DOO. Well then you gotta do something even more drastic. Like rent a balloon or something.

VINCENT. Balloon?

DOO-DOO. Yeah, big balloon. One of those terigibles there.

VINCENT. What?

DOO-DOO. Terigibles, the blimp.

VINCENT. Dirigible.

DOO-DOO. Whatever. You get a big one, you rent it. And you have it painted with big words, I'm Sorry, Please Marry Me, Come Back Soon, Or I'm Gonna Start Looking Like This Fucking Blimp 'cause I've eaten every cannoli from here to Little Italy. Something like that.

VINCENT. Nah, it's gotta be something...I gotta make it up to her. Somehow.

DOO-DOO. You gotta give her diamonds or flowers, something like that.

VINCENT. No.

DOO-DOO. Something she loves.

VINCENT. What?

DOO-DOO. Something she loves. What does she love more than anything?

VINCENT. Acting, I guess.

DOO-DOO. Then you gotta give her a part in something.

VINCENT. I already tried to do that. Look where it got me.

DOO-DOO. Yeah. Too bad. The way you used to carry on with all that casting stuff, I woulda believed you were one of those, how you call it, industry insider guys.

VINCENT. Really.

DOO-DOO. Yeah. Coulda had me fooled.

VINCENT. Wait a minute. Stay there, hold on.

(All at once, he grabs the phone.)

DOO-DOO. What?

VINCENT. This might work. Yeah, uh, I need the number of the Utah Shakespeare Festival. Right Utah, like the Jazz.

DOO-DOO. What are you doing?

VINCENT. I'm gonna get her a part in *Othello*. And then I'm going to go down to that diner and give her the good news.

DOO-DOO. Bring her some cannolis. That way you don't eat 'em all.

VINCENT. Edie wants an audition, I'll get her an audition. *(Into the phone.)* Hello, Utah Shakespeare Festival? This is Vincent DiDonato, of Centennial Casting.

(Blackout.)

Scene Four – The Office

(CARMINE and DOO-DOO are having a heated discussion in the office. DOO-DOO sweeps the floor.)

DOO-DOO. So he's on the phone and he's got this casting guy, Lance, eating out of his hand.

CARMINE. You're kidding.

DOO-DOO. No. I heard him. He was talking the pants off the guy. But he got Edie an audition. Her own private audition.

CARMINE. Outstanding.

DOO-DOO. That is very hard to do. This is akin to a screen test.

CARMINE. So he's down there now?

DOO-DOO. He went to the diner to give her the good news. He even brought her a congratulatory box of cannolis!

CARMINE. Edie will be so pleased.

(The door opens, revealing a slightly injured VINCENT, holding a large napkin wrapped around a very small wound on his hand. He's not bleeding, but his pride is hurt.)

DOO-DOO. Vinnie!

VINCENT. She stuck a fork in me.

DOO-DOO. Edie?

VINCENT. No, that nutjob friend of hers, Michele. She hit me with a pan and then she stuck me with a fork.

CARMINE. Why did she do that?

DOO-DOO. She wanted to see if he was done.

(DOO-DOO laughs and keeps laughing until VINCENT catches him. He stops and puts on the "serious" look, as if to understand the real tragedy at work.)

VINCENT. Ha ha.

CARMINE. Did you tell Edie about the audition?

VINCENT. I didn't even get to see Edie.

DOO-DOO. Well, you gotta go back there.

VINCENT. Are you nuts? Her friend will castrate me with a butter knife.

CARMINE. You gotta tell her about the audition.

VINCENT. Forget about it. She freakin' hates me.

DOO-DOO. Ah, come on Vin –

CARMINE. If you just had a chance to talk to her –

VINCENT. She ain't gonna talk to me. She don't wanna see me again. Ever.

DOO-DOO. Vinnie –

VINCENT. *(Rising.)* Never mind. I'm through. The whole thing was a stupid idea anyway. I lied to her. She found out. It's over.

(He exits onto the shop floor.)

(Pause. **CARMINE** *and* **DOO-DOO** *share a look.)*

DOO-DOO. Well. That's that.

*(***CARMINE** *begins sobbing quietly.)*

Aw, don't start Carmine.

CARMINE. I'm sorry.

DOO-DOO. Forget about it. Let's have a cannoli.

CARMINE. Those were for Edie.

DOO-DOO. Well, evidently she didn't want 'em.

*(***DOO-DOO** *begins opening the box.)*

CARMINE. *(Still crying.)* But they were destined to be lovers.

DOO-DOO. The only thing they're destined for is – whoa, what's this?

(He opens the box and pulls out stacks of postcards.)

CARMINE. *(Reading.)* Sequoia Gallery, Contemporary Metal Sculptures.

(Suddenly, **MICHELE** *booms through the door, furious.)*

MICHELE. HEY! HAND OVER THE BOX!

DOO-DOO. What?

MICHELE. Is this Centennial Casting?

DOO-DOO. Yeah.

MICHELE. What a dump! When your dopey boss left the diner, he took the wrong box.

(She walks up and tries to grab the box from **DOO-DOO***, who holds on.)*

DOO-DOO. Hey, hold on.

MICHELE. Those are the postcards for my show. Here's your stinking cannolis.

CARMINE. You know, perhaps you could use some anger management classes.

MICHELE. Here's how I manage my anger! *(Brandishing a fork.)*

CARMINE. Give her the box.

DOO-DOO. Now just calm down.

CARMINE. Doo-Doo, she's got a fork!

MICHELE. Doo-Doo? Oh, I heard about you. You're the director guy.

DOO-DOO. And you must be the enticing best friend –

MICHELE. Yeah, yeah. Save it for your movie.

DOO-DOO. Look, I'm not afraid of you! And I'm not afraid of your silverware!

MICHELE. Hand 'em over!

(Holding the box of cannolis in one hand and the fork in the other.)

DOO-DOO. Let me explain something. Vinnie didn't mean to –

MICHELE. I don't care what he did or didn't mean. Just give me the postcards! I'm double-parked!!

EDIE. *(Pokes her head through the door.)* Pssst. Mish, are you okay?

MICHELE. *(Brandishing the fork for emphasis, to* **EDIE**.*)* You, get in the car.

(To **DOO-DOO**.*)* You, give me those cards!

(To **CARMINE**.*)* You, stay put!

DOO-DOO. Carmine, go get Vinnie!

> *(She points the fork at* **DOO-DOO**'*s crotch,* **CARMINE** *does not move.)*

Now!

> *(***CARMINE** *exits.)*

MICHELE. Oh jeez, give me the frigging cards!

DOO-DOO. He needs to talk to her.

MICHELE. He wants to talk to somebody, he can talk to me.

> *(***MICHELE** *grabs the cards.)*

VINCENT. *(Enters, dragged on by* **CARMINE**.*)* What?! What?! What is it?

> *(He sees* **MICHELE** *brandishing the fork.)*

Oh. Whoa...

EDIE. I got nothing to say. Let's go.

> *(***EDIE** *and* **MICHELE** *head for the door.)*

VINCENT. Edie, I got you an audition.

> *(***EDIE** *and* **MICHELE** *stop, look at each other.)*

EDIE. An audition?

VINCENT. Yeah.

EDIE. *(To* **MICHELE**.*)* You believe this?

MICHELE. An audition for what? How to be an Asshole, Part Two?

EDIE. You know, after all the bullshit he puts me through, making me look stupid, so he could have a good laugh with his friends –

VINCENT. That's not –

EDIE. – He comes waltzing over to me and does he say "I'm sorry, I didn't mean to hurt your feelings, I was wrong"?

VINCENT. I am sorry.

EDIE. No, he tries to pull the same stunt again.

MICHELE. Unbelievable.

EDIE. It is unbelievable. Like I'm some kind of bimbo who'll do anything to get a part. What happened?
(*To* **DOO-DOO**.) You want to dress up like a German director this time?

MICHELE. That's it. It's a romantic comedy set on a German submarine, Das Love Boot.

EDIE. Yeah. I could be the captain –

VINCENT. It's for *Othello*.

EDIE. Yeah, right.

MICHELE. Where's it playing, your basement?

VINCENT. The Utah Shakespeare Festival. They're in town next week.

DOO-DOO. He ain't kidding. I heard him make the call.

(*Pause.*)

EDIE. Mish, give me a second here, would ya?

MICHELE. What are you doing?

EDIE. Nothing.

MICHELE. This guy don't deserve the time of day.

EDIE. Glass booth! Just for one minute.
(*To* **VINCENT**.) I'm gonna...

VINCENT. I'm sorry, Edie. I'm so sorry I hurt you. I just wanted to meet you.

EDIE. So you had to go through all this bullshit? Setting up all this, what, all these scenarios...why?

VINCENT. The whole thing got out of control. I thought eventually I would find the right time to tell you. But then we would get together and you would talk about your acting and I thought...I thought you were only interested in me 'cause I was some casting director.

EDIE. What about going to the track and the dinners and the shows? Vincent, we had a good time.

VINCENT. I know.

EDIE. Did you think I was so shallow that I'd only date you so you could get me an acting job?

VINCENT. No. I guess I just didn't think there was that much to me.

EDIE. On top of that, you never even got me a frigging job.

VINCENT. I know, that's what this is. I wanted to make it up to you. See –

> (*He reaches into his pocket for a piece of paper.*)

EDIE. I don't want to know.

VINCENT. This is a real audition.

EDIE. If you think for one minute –

VINCENT. It's for Emilia in *Othello*.

EDIE. – That I'm gonna fall for your –

VINCENT. Listen, you wanted to play Desdemona, but you're right for Emilia. See Desdemona's good, but Emilia's been kicked around too and finally at the end...she finds the courage to stand up to the guy, you know? I could see you playing a part like that. Anyway, I called the guy and got you an audition.

EDIE. Who?

VINCENT. Lance, that was the casting guy's name. I called him up and told him about you, how you're a great actress and he should see you, so he set up a time for you. See?

EDIE. You got blood on it.

VINCENT. She stuck me with a fork.

> (**EDIE** *looks at* **MICHELE**.)

MICHELE. Sorry.

VINCENT. Hey, I told Lance I believed in you. I figured that had to be good for something. Anyway, that's it. If I were you, I'd go down, give it a shot.

EDIE. What's the point? *(Starts to leave.)*

VINCENT. Edie –

EDIE. I quit the business.

VINCENT. You can't! We broke the curse!

EDIE. Evidently not.

VINCENT. No, wait. Listen! When I first got into casting –

EDIE. This oughta be good.

VINCENT. No, not casting, I mean, casting.

> *(He points to the room.)*

This kinda casting. When I used to work with my father, all he did was yell at me all the time, 'cause whatever I did, it was never good enough for him. And casting is pretty simple, right? You melt the metal and you pour it in and you wait and it pops out and it's always the same. Except when I did it, I was always afraid I'd get it wrong. And I did. I'd pour in too much or too little and it never came out right. Never. So one day I told my mother, that was it, I couldn't do this no more. And she said, "Vincent, you gotta stop thinking about what it's gonna look like in the end, and just do the work. Do the pouring and the setting and don't worry about the mold."

EDIE. What does that have to do with me?

> *(Pause as **VINCENT** tries to find the right words.)*

VINCENT. Stop worrying about whether they like you or not. Just do your work. See, Emilia's the mold, right? Just fill her up. Like only you can do. Okay?

EDIE. Vincent, don't you get it? After what you did to me, I've got nothing to fill her up with. I'm empty.

> *(She exits. **VINCENT** watches her go.)*

VINCENT. *(To the boys.)* All right, that's it.

> *(**VINCENT** exits.)*

DOO-DOO. *(To* **MICHELE**.*)* I know you beat up Vinnie, but you really should've been beating up me. 'Cause I was the one who set up the date with Edie in the first place. I mean, Vinnie, he took one look at Edie's picture and he was over the moon.

MICHELE. All right, Edie don't even know this, but *I'm* the one who sent in the stupid pictures in the first place. She had all these old headshots she was gonna throw out, and I figured that was a waste. So as a gift, I sent them out for her. Only trouble was, I didn't know how to find the addresses for the casting places, so I looked in the yellow pages.

CARMINE. Under Casting! An honest mistake.

MICHELE. Thanks.

DOO-DOO. Jeez, what a disaster.

MICHELE. Yeah. Look, I gotta go.

CARMINE. Uh, excuse me, miss?

MICHELE. What?

CARMINE. *(Holding a postcard.)* I couldn't help but notice your postcard. Did you weld this dragonfly arrangement?

MICHELE. Yeah, that's me.

CARMINE. Very impressive work. It's poetry in metal.

MICHELE. Thanks.

CARMINE. This is aluminum, correct?

MICHELE. For the original, yeah. But I'm supposed to do another one made of cast iron.

CARMINE. Oooh, that is challenging. Keeps falling apart, right?

MICHELE. *(This stops her.)* Yeah. How did you know?

CARMINE. Cast iron is considered a dirty metal. You have to braze it.

MICHELE. Huh?

CARMINE. What you need is a good brass flux and a hard solder.

MICHELE. Really?

DOO-DOO. Maybe Carmine could help you out. He's pretty good at it, Michele.

CARMINE. Michele. That's Vinnie's mother's name.

> (**CARMINE** *blushes visibly. And it seems as if his crying days are over...*)

DOO-DOO. Michele, I'll make a deal with you. We'll give you a hand with your dragonfly and you give us a hand getting these two crazy kids back together.

MICHELE. Oh yeah? And how are we gonna do that?

DOO-DOO. Let's just say we all get together and we do a little...brazing.

> (*They look at* **DOO-DOO***, they look at each other.*)
>
> (*Blackout.*)

Scene Five – The Track

ANNOUNCER. *(Voice-over.)* Results from race number seven, Loosey Goosey to win, Eat My Hat to place, and to show, Big Fat Liar.

> *(The track on a Saturday afternoon.* **CARMINE** *and* **DOO-DOO** *stand at the rail, on either side of* **VINCENT**, *looking through the racing forms.)*

DOO-DOO. What do you like this time?

CARMINE. Uhhh...I like...Slo Go Mo.

DOO-DOO. Slo Go Mo...Carmine, it's forty to one.

CARMINE. So?

DOO-DOO. This frigging horse hasn't won anything in years.

CARMINE. I feel sorry for her. She's probably due.

DOO-DOO. She's overdue, for the glue factory. All right, I like Singapore Cat. Two bucks.

> *(***CARMINE** *hands some money to* **DOO-DOO**.*)*

Who do you like, Vinnie? Vinnie?

VINCENT. What?

DOO-DOO. You betting this race?

VINCENT. Oh sorry. Which race is this?

DOO-DOO. Number four. Come on, get with the program.

VINCENT. *(Looking at the program.)* All right, what do we got here...

CARMINE. What time is it?

VINCENT. 12:45.

CARMINE. 12:45. It's 12:45, Doo-Doo.

> *(He gives* **DOO-DOO** *a big wink.)*

VINCENT. And in one minute it'll be 12:46. Who cares?

> *(He hands* **DOO-DOO** *some money.)*

Here, give me two bucks on the seven horse to win. What the hell you looking around for?

DOO-DOO. Nothing, I thought I saw somebody I knew.

CARMINE. Tuck in your shirt, boss. I think it's more slimming.

> *(He starts to tuck in* **VINCENT***'s shirt for him.)*

VINCENT. Get your hands off me –

> *(***DOO-DOO** *joins in the grooming of* **VINCENT***.)*

DOO-DOO. You got schmutz on your collar.

VINCENT. What the – What's the matter with you guys? You better get going, the window's gonna close.

DOO-DOO. All right. It's nice here, you know? I ain't been to the track in years.

VINCENT. Yeah. I used to come here with Edie.

> *(Pause.)*

I miss her.

CARMINE. We all do.

VINCENT. I wonder how she's doing.

DOO-DOO. Why don't you ask her?

VINCENT. Huh?

> *(***EDIE** *and* **MICHELE** *enter.)*

EDIE. Well.

VINCENT. Edie.

DOO-DOO. Fancy meeting you here!

EDIE. Michele...you said we were meeting your son.

MICHELE. Yeah.

DOO-DOO. This was my idea, Miss Keaton. I take full responsibility. Vinnie didn't know anything about it. Did you, Vin? Vinnie?

VINCENT. *(To* **EDIE***.)* How you doing?

EDIE. I'm good, Vincent.

MICHELE. I'm sorry, hon. I hope you're not mad.

EDIE. No, no.

DOO-DOO. Oooh, getting close to post time.

> *(To* **CARMINE** *and* **MICHELE***.)* All right, what do you say we go place some bets and buy a couple of dogs? You in Michele?

MICHELE. Sure.

(*To* **EDIE.**) Be right back, hon.

DOO-DOO. All right, let's go.

MICHELE. And by the way, Carmine, that brazing you did for me? Like butter.

CARMINE. It was a pleasure. And may I say, I have never seen such beauty in alloys.

MICHELE. I got some more work for you...if you're interested.

CARMINE. I got a blowtorch and I know how to use it.

> (**CARMINE** *and* **MICHELE** *exit, arm in arm, followed by* **DOO-DOO.**)

VINCENT. I had nothing to do with this.

EDIE. Sure.

VINCENT. You gotta believe me.

EDIE. I do.

VINCENT. Nice day huh?

EDIE. Yep.

VINCENT. Nothing like a day at the track. Jeez, if it wasn't for you, I'd still be watching 'em run on the screens at OTB.

EDIE. Smells better out here too.

VINCENT. Yeah.

EDIE. Look, I should thank you. Utah liked my work and I'm going out there to be an understudy.

VINCENT. So what, you got it?

EDIE. No, an understudy. For Emilia. It's paying work, I might get to go on now and then. It's a long season, you know? Six months.

VINCENT. Hey, that's great.

EDIE. And I was thinking while I was out there, maybe once I get settled, I could maybe see the West Coast a little, LA.

VINCENT. Jeez, that's wonderful. Hey, I knew you had it in you.

EDIE. You did. Even when I didn't. You know, it sounds funny, but that mold thing you told me, I think it really helped.

VINCENT. Ah, you probably would have got it anyway.

(*Pause.*)

EDIE. Look, I gotta go. I'm not even packed and I'm supposed to fly out Sunday night.

VINCENT. Oh. Well that's...hey, the important thing is you got it. And now...you're on your way, right?

EDIE. Right.

VINCENT. And uh...jeez, it's good to see you smile. Hey, I'm sorry I hurt you. But I gotta say, I'm not sorry this happened. Just that it happened the way it did, you know?

EDIE. Well, it all worked out.

VINCENT. Yeah, but that was mean. I shouldn't have done it.

EDIE. Hey, maybe you should get into casting.

VINCENT. You think?

EDIE. You got me a gig, right?

VINCENT. Ah, what do I know about the theatre? I own Centennial Casting. We make fittings, moldings, cheap car parts. That's who I am and that's all I'll ever be. You know, I think Carmine's right. Maybe we should computerize, get into the twentieth century, you know? Clean the place up a bit. It's about time I got out of the plating room and started running that shop.

EDIE. Sure.

(*Pause.*)

Look, I didn't care if you were a big deal casting person. It didn't mean anything to me. I just liked being with you.

VINCENT. (*Nods.*) Funny how things work out, you know?

EDIE. What?

VINCENT. Like, when you really do something for somebody, something really good for them, from the heart, it ends up taking them away from you.

(Pause.)

You know, I never been west of Weehawken.

EDIE. There's a whole big world out there.

VINCENT. They got racetracks in Utah?

EDIE. Nah. Just a lot of salt.

(Pause.)

I can't stick around. Let me go find Mish.

(She starts to walk away.)

VINCENT. Edie...

EDIE. Yeah?

VINCENT. Stay a while. We gotta celebrate a little at least.

EDIE. Oh I don't –

VINCENT. I bet the last race. You gotta watch with me.

EDIE. I can't.

VINCENT. Tell you what, just look at the program and see if you can guess who I bet. Let's see if I learned anything here.

EDIE. Well, "Big Fat Liar" already ran.

VINCENT. Come on. Just take a look. You always knew how to pick 'em.

EDIE. Let me see.

(She takes the program.)

Okay. Knowing you, I think you put some money on... *(Laughs.)* ..."Truth Be Told"?

VINCENT. You got it. "Truth Be Told." See? Likes a slow track, hasn't won in a while. I figure his luck is due to change. And he's got a lot of heart.

EDIE. That's got to count for something.

(The bell rings and the race has begun.)

VINCENT. Oops, there they go.

(They turn to the track and watch. Pause.)

EDIE. I love to watch 'em run.

VINCENT. He looks pretty good, right?

EDIE. Yeah. A little rough coming out of the gate, but he might do okay.

VINCENT. Now let's see how he finishes.

> *(**EDIE** has rested her hand on top of the rail. The two barely focus on the race, not knowing what to say to each other, or what will happen next. **VINCENT** looks at **EDIE**, but **EDIE** looks straight ahead. He then looks straight out at the track and no one knows if they'll end up together. We hear the race continue and the crowd noises swell as the lights fade to black.)*

End of Play